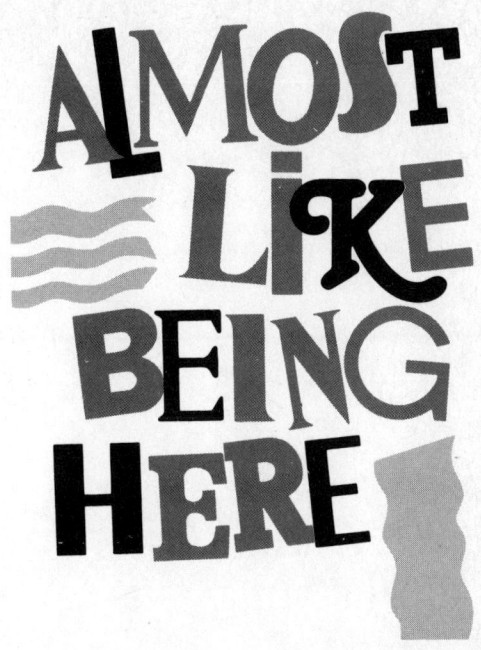

TOM LEOPOLD

ALMOST LIKE BEING HERE

E. P. DUTTON  NEW YORK

Copyright © 1988 by Tom Leopold
All rights reserved. Printed in the U.S.A.

PUBLISHER'S NOTE: *This novel is a work of fiction. Names, characters, places, and incidents either are the product of the author's imagination or are used fictitiously, and any resemblance to actual persons, living or dead, events, or locales is entirely coincidental.*

No part of this publication may be reproduced or transmitted in any form or by any means, electronic or mechanical, including photocopy, recording, or any information storage and retrieval system now known or to be invented, without permission in writing from the publisher, except by a reviewer who wishes to quote brief passages in connection with a review written for inclusion in a magazine, newspaper, or broadcast.

Published in the United States by E. P. Dutton, a division of NAL Penguin Inc., 2 Park Avenue, New York, N.Y. 10016.

Published simultaneously in Canada by Fitzhenry and Whiteside, Limited, Toronto.

Library of Congress Cataloging-in-Publication Data
Leopold, Tom.
Almost like being here / Tom Leopold. — 1st ed.
p. cm.
ISBN: 0-525-24632-0
I. Title.
PS3562.E59A79 1988   87-30704
813'.54—dc19   CIP

Designed by REM Studios

1 3 5 7 9 10 8 6 4 2

First Edition

For my father in memory,
and my mother, in Miami.

I want to thank my pal Oliver Clark for
listening to me talk about it so much,
and for his good suggestions.
I want to thank my three brothers and Barbara.
Mostly I'd like to thank my friend and editor,
Margaret Blackstone. She made it a better book.

"Why should I modulate when
I am perfectly happy in the tonality I'm in?"

—Claude Achille Debussy
(At age eleven to his music teacher)

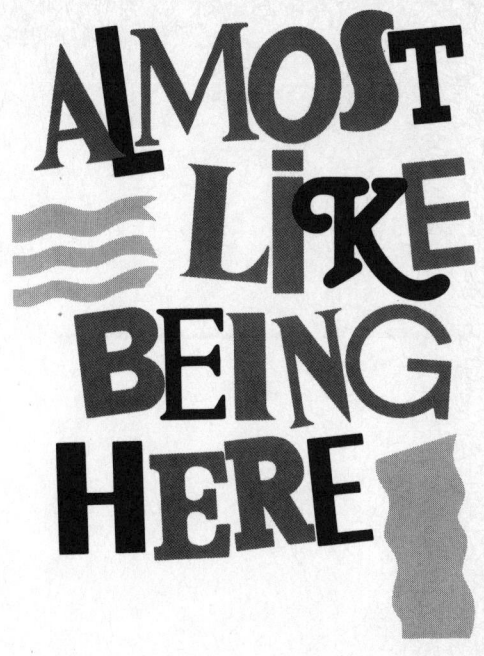

MONDAY

A while back I got a phone call from Mary's longtime boyfriend. The one she left for me and then went back to after me. I had never met him, although once I did see him and Mary huddling in a doorway on Fifth Avenue during a rainstorm. He was trying to hail the cab I was riding in. There was a second where I figured I'd tell the driver to pull over, and I'd give them a lift. Honestly, I didn't do it only because he might have been pissed off meeting me.

Surprisingly, I wouldn't have felt uncomfortable meeting Ansil. Not that I would have had a right to. But that's never stopped anybody. Mary also would have had the whole night to act like she wasn't noticing how totally normal we were both acting.

When she would describe him to me, he sounded a lot like the old me, which is still me only I've stopped getting into those situations.

Anyway, the crux of the phone call was that Mary had succeeded in killing herself. She was now dead and the boyfriend didn't know why, but he wanted to tell me before anyone else did.

"We buried her two days ago," he said. "She was in Boston for her father's birthday. She died right there on the grounds."

Apparently everybody got through toasting the old man around ten o'clock and then she went upstairs and swallowed the last fourteen thousand Placidyls of her life. Then she took the back stairs out of the main house, went to the pool house, which was next to the playhouse, went to sleep, and died. Her brother, Jake, found her.

Mary and I took Jake out to dinner one night. He had a terrible stutter. He was always going off camping or climbing mountains by himself. Mary told me that when Oxford College invited him to enroll, their father had had to hire a gang of backwoods detectives to track him down. I overheard a conversation Mary and her brother had in my kitchen the next morning while I was still in bed. After a second I realized he was hardly stuttering at all.

All I knew about their father was that he was a moody old doctor at Harvard who used to find cures for diseases by day and get drunk and dangle his two kids out of the upstairs window by night.

When Mary discussed her mother it was always with a tone of admiration in her voice. So much so that you almost didn't hear her or it didn't register when she told you that her mother had run out on them when Mary was eleven. I'd met her mother once too. After Mary grew up, her mother started popping back into her life.

Now, you know me. It's not exactly my style to slap women around, but I thought this woman was maybe the worst person on the planet, not that the old man sounded much better. I didn't hit her though. I wasn't even cold to her, because it would have been like behaving that way to Mary.

There was a long pause on both ends of the phone. I was glad the boyfriend had called, but apart from that the rest of my feelings were outside myself, in different parts of the room. Mary's boyfriend didn't "know what else to say." There was quiet on the line, and having not uttered one word since hello, I said, "How are *you*? How've you been taking it?"

There was a pause again and then he said, "Not good. I'm not good."

"Look," I said, "you live down in SoHo, right?" Mary had told me he did.

"That's right."

"Well, you know? What are you doing around ten-thirty or something? What are you doing around then, Ansil?" Mary had told me his name when she and I first started seeing each other and I used to kid her, never having seen her ex, about what he must look like. I'd tell her, "I bet Ansil's like six-foot-six with that bad electric red hair, the kinky variety, and I bet he's got one long, red hair sticking out of the side of his neck." From then until the time we were no longer together I referred to him as "Big Red."

I made a date to meet Ansil at ten-thirty at the Broome Street Bar. I don't know why. I suppose I thought it was important to hear more about Mary. I had been getting dressed for work when he called. When I hung up the phone I fell all around the living room trying to get my other leg into my pants.

We buried her two days ago.

I couldn't yet know what I felt. It was as if a gun had gone off next to me and I was checking myself for holes.

I walked out of my apartment and was locking the door when coincidentally, as usual, Pilar's door opened at the end of the hall. Pilar is a twenty-two- to twenty-four-year-old actress who moved into my building at the behest of Ricky Lupone, a ham radio freak, who had lived there for years. Ricky always had a red bandanna on his head and a hammer hanging off his pants. Pilar is the total actress. If you meet her in the hall, she's acting. If you get a laugh out of her, she's acting. But it's only when she's acting you can *really* tell she's acting. She finally drove Ricky out of the building. About a year ago she knocked on my door to borrow my stapler to staple a picture of herself to something and I was drunk and I don't have to tell you what happened then. We're all adults here.

I regret the incident for a couple of reasons. One, while we were doing the "Patrice Lumumba," as I like to call it, on the couch, an actress she hated, who is actually a good actress, came on TV. I'm not certain about our positioning, but I think her legs were wrapped around my head or something. She asked me what I thought of this actress and I said I thought she was good. Well, with that, Pilar got up and started to argue about it, sending a mediocre lay into the crapper. My other reason for regretting that night is that Pilar has "just happened" to run into me in the hall about six million times since. I know I should be flattered, but I'm not, okay?

"Hi, Sandy," Pilar said as we met at the stairway. She was taking her laundry down at seven at night.

"Hi, Pilar."

"You going up to the theater?"

"Yeah," I said.

"You still getting good houses?" she asked.

"Yeah, I guess so. I suppose we are. I dunno."

She asked me if I'd read the flyer she'd slid under my door. Even though she's straight she was always appearing in lesbian plays in theaters with names like "The Lesbo Women's Coalition Alliance Anti-Sperm Workshop Theater Lab."

"I don't think I can come see it, Pilar. I think my play runs the same hours as yours, doesn't it?" I said.

"We do a two A.M. show and serve champagne and eggs. You could make that," she said.

Now, I know I have a lot of growing up to do, but somehow I don't want to sit in a twelve-seat theater at two A.M. and have twenty fat actresses holler at me from the stage about my sexism and then have to eat their eggs.

"Well, slip another flyer under my door, Pilar, and I'll try to make it."

It was pretty cold out on the street. It was early January and there were record low temperatures every second. I stood on the corner of West Eleventh and Hudson for a full minute and couldn't remember why I was standing there or why I was waving my arms. A cab finally pulled up and I got in.

"Forty-ninth Street and Eighth Avenue, please. The right side of the street."

The black driver nodded his head. He had his hair in that style where chunks of it are tied off into octopus arms separated by beads.

I had worked in this show on Broadway for five

and a half months. The play is about a Mafia summit meeting in Atlantic City. It was a big comedy hit although it was shit. It was scheduled to close the second week in February. It wasn't doing bad business, but this crazy Spanish furniture heiress who put all the money into the thing had decided to close the show prematurely after the director called her a cunt at a party in East Hampton. So the director calls her a cunt and I'm out of work. I think that's fair.

My function in the production was to run in during the last six seconds of the show in a cop's uniform and arrest one of the Mafia guys who is hiding out in a *La Cage Aux Folles*-type nightclub chorus line. And that's when the laughs really begin. For this I cleared a few hundred dollars a week. My real job, however, was to stand by for the role of Dink, a hired assassin who has tracked the Mafioso and identifies him, even though he's posing as Liza Minnelli. This part was played by Victor Sprigger who is not the world's best actor. He never got sick so I've never had to go on and play the part. Now, I'm not such a great actor myself, but I'm funnier than Victor is. But he's better looking—tall, blond. Actually, he looks like a better-looking version of me. It was difficult enough coming to the theater every night prepared to do the part, because you have to keep yourself psyched up just in case, and then to see Victor come running in late every night, that strains your nerves. About two months into the run I started getting painful boils under the skin of my shoulders. A very attractive look.

Mary had waited with me backstage a couple of times. No more than twice, yet for a long time afterwards people would ask me how Mary was doing or if anyone was publishing her stories yet. Real concerned, too. She was such a strange combination. She was beautiful—small, old-fashioned, cameo-brooch beautiful—with hair black and soft, puffed full of air and swirled on top of her head. White skin and violet eyes. Real *violet* eyes, with tiny veins of a turquoise color on the lids. And it was there that the tale was told. The eyes made you want to look after her. Sometimes you could see them drift, as if she were seeing you through the wrong end of a telescope. It was as if someone inside her head came up to her as she stood in front of the window she was seeing you from, and led her away.

Mary once sat next to me in the basement of the theater during one of our regular poker games. It may sound like I'm making this up, but I swear I won every hand for close to an hour. I usually never win. The guys pretended they were enraged at her presence. It got very funny and nice because everyone caught on to her. And Mary would laugh too. I'd get on a roll every now and then, and really get her going, laughing like a hungry man at a banquet. She was starved for laughter.

I checked the sign-in sheet near the theater door. Victor's name had a check by it, so that meant I'd be sitting on my ass till the end of the show. It would be great if he died and I had to go on. But that scumbag would never die. So I might as well give up hoping for it.

I went down to my friend Tony's dressing room. He's a real nice, funny person of the homo-American school. He's effeminate and tough at the same time. Funny guy, Tony. Bitter funny. Sarcastic. Which is the best. I wanted to see if he had any speed. He always had drugs. I pretty well had stopped with that kind of stuff, but right then I couldn't seem to keep myself from asking.

"I just have downs. You can have some of those," Tony said.

"Nah, that's okay, Tony."

He was standing on a chair Velcroing red balloons to himself. During a musical number at the end of the show Tony pops the balloons with a pin while singing "Life Is Just a Bowl of Cherries." For this people were paying fifty dollars a seat.

"I'm going to be buying a little cocaine after the show. I could get you some of that," he whispered.

"No thanks," I said. "Two minutes after I snort cocaine I'm up all night sitting on the edge of the bed waiting for the Nazis to come."

"Hand me the eyebrow pencil, darling. I forgot my eyes."

I handed it up to him. His makeup table was furnished like a little home. Framed pictures, good luck mementos, even a red velour towel upon which his makeup was laid. One of his balloons popped. I handed him another.

"Thank you, Sandy. You're a good woman," he said. Tony refers to every man as a woman. "Oh, darling, the President is not a happy woman about this Arab situation." Tony lives down in the Village too. Sometimes we'll take the subway down to Fourteenth Street or Sheridan Square together. I've gotten past the point where I'm worried that he'll grab my rig. We've become pretty good friends.

We were riding the train when Tony told me about his childhood in a violent neighborhood in Manhattan.

"You had to be tough to be a queen where I grew up," he said. "People frowned on that sort of activity. The mentality of the guys I grew up with was flexible. They hated fags, but to get even with them, to really teach them a lesson, a gang of the toughest kids would beat up a couple of the Nellies and fuck 'em in the ass just to show 'em they couldn't pull that fag stuff around their neighborhood."

Tony was putting the last purple sparkles around

his eyes when the stage manager stuck his head in the door.

"You didn't sign in on the call sheet, Tony," he said.

Tony stomped his foot and replied, "I'm an artist, not a circus freak. Knock next time."

Tony carefully sat down and lit a cigarette. "What's bothering you, Sandelino?" he asked.

I told him that I was just depressed in a general way. Tony said that nobody was ever depressed in a general way.

"Take George Sanders," he said. "He left a suicide note saying that he was bored and that was the reason. But she was lying, Miss Sanders. She was broke, her wife had recently died, and she had recently had a small stroke."

"What are you saying, Tony?" I said. "That I'm depressed because George Sanders's wife died?"

That got a mild laugh and then Tony looked genuinely concerned, which made me feel guilty.

"A friend of mine tried to kill himself," I said. "Everything's fine but it did fuck me up to a certain degree. It's someone I haven't seen for a while but it's distressing, you know."

A few years before, when I started feeling better about myself, I began lying to make life more comfortable. In the case of Mary's death I was confused, so I was keeping a close watch on myself. I was thirteen when one of my grandfathers died. I started crying when my father told me the news and then I went into the bathroom, locked the door, and watched myself in the mirror to see what I looked like crying. I'm a little on the self-centered side, you see. So telling Tony about Mary at that point only would have been requesting something for myself. And who was I? I wasn't the one who was dead here.

When I phased back in I heard Tony telling me that "If only people who committed suicide could look back through the keyhole and see that people they wanted to get even with didn't spend the rest of their lives mourning over them, they never would do it."

He's right about that. But Mary was no jerk. And from what I remembered about her, ego had nothing to do with it.

I guided Tony down to the greenroom so his costume wouldn't pop. I had an hour before I had to go on stage to do some of that fine acting work I do. I thought about going to a porno movie for forty minutes or so. I hadn't gone to one in a couple of years. I love when people tell me that pornography repels them. Now, I certainly don't think people should be allowed to make dirty films with children in them. There's nothing sexy about a four-year-old girl and a goat anyway. But if people say that seeing great-looking people fucking doesn't excite them, they're clearly lying. And you know me, you know how I feel about lying.

When I first moved to New York from Miami I went to porno houses all the time. I was so nervous and crazy, pornos and sleep were the only things that stopped me from thinking. At eleven in the morning I'd be sitting there in some jizz-infected seat watching *Donkey Lunch* or *Wet Teenagers* or something. The audience for those movies usually consisted of me, the odd wino who wasn't looking at the screen, and a group of twenty or thirty well-dressed Japanese businessmen. At every porno house it was the same thing. I figured two things: either the Japs are mobilizing again, and this was where they made their war plans, or they'd flown halfway around the world just to see films with blonde or red-headed pussies in them. Six-foot women with blonde pussies. The concept drives them nuts. Tours are organized. Buses chartered.

I decided against it. Mary was dead. Watching people fuck couldn't get at that.

I remembered I'd planned to meet Ansil downtown after the show. I wondered what that was going to be like. It was a potential Truffaut film. Me as Jean-Louis Trintignant. I'm so like him in every way. Except I don't look anything like him, I'm twenty years younger, and I don't speak French, or, for that matter, any language, fluently. A *Jules and Jim* kind of thing. It was a this; it was a that.

There was a costume girl at the theater I was seeing. Ann. Cute, blonde, a nice girl, wonderful dresser. (Sounds like I'm trying to fix you up with her.) After Mary, because it was such a good thing, I tried to date only girls I liked. That sounds dumb, I know, because the premise of dating, you'd figure, is seeing people you like. But it doesn't seem as if people do that. A lot of the time people fall in love and at a certain point the affair becomes all about worrying who the other person is fucking. Or trying to get yourself back to the person you were when she was still impressed with you.

Don't get mad at me. I could be wrong.

But I liked Mary. I loved her. And when it didn't work out for us, because of what we thought was bad timing, the end had goodwill in it. She wasn't through with the love affair she'd had before me, and I was relieved. I had begun to feel bad. We liked what we had enough not to ruin it by overstaying our welcome. We said. It was a good love affair. We said.

A friend once asked me about a female friend of mine and whether we were sleeping together. I said, "We're just friends." And he said, "Who do you sleep with, your enemies?"

I'd been staying up at this girl Ann's place a couple of times a week. I have a loft bed down at my apartment, and Ann hated sleeping on it. "The ceiling's gonna lower down on me in the night and crush me like in an Edgar Allan Poe poem," she'd say.

As it turned out, Ann knew people who knew me. The first night we went out after the show I took her to Sardi's. I like the deviled beef bones there. She told me I had a bad reputation.

"My friends say you love 'em and leave 'em," she said.

All of a sudden I was in a John Garfield movie. I had probably once slept with a girlfriend of hers who thought I took advantage of her by taking her out for a good dinner and a movie, then for drinks, then going to her apartment after being invited, making love, and having a good time, but not asking her out again because I wasn't that interested. Therefore, I achieved lousehood.

To find out if you like anybody you have to go out with them. But if you feel you don't want to pursue it after that, you've used them. This is not always the case, although I have, in fact, used my share of people. As you head toward thirty and you don't live with anyone or see anyone for any great length of time, you become more attractive to women around your age or older. So I don't have to do a lot of fancy stuff to get laid. Consequently I try to be fairly legit about things. But there is no way of winning. You cannot win.

I guess it sounds vain to draw this conclusion because maybe Ann already liked me and really didn't want me to love her and leave her. And just hearing what her friend had said would probably make me want to prove them both wrong. But I was into this new thing. I like to call it Not Having a Miserable Life. So if I hadn't wanted to call her friend again I wouldn't have, taking the risk of adding to my growing legend as a shit-heel. But I did like Ann.

"You have a joint or something, Ann?" She was ironing somebody's dance belt or something, down in the wardrobe room of the theater. Her parents were keeping her in a great apartment near Bloomingdale's. She had a fine collection of classical music up there. One thing I enjoyed was having a cup of coffee in the morning at Ann's place. Bach on the stereo. I'd gaze out at the guys unloading Vuitton bags from their trucks, winter steam blowing out of their noses. I like to be in an all-girl place sometimes. I'm getting to think that if I ever do get married I'd have to opt for an unorthodox type of marriage where the husband lives alone and comes over for a date with his wife once or twice a week. I like an all-feminine environment on a semi-regular basis in the same way I like to go to a married couple's house for dinner now and then. No, that's not true. I hate that.

Ann didn't have a joint with her. She also seemed mad at me.

"Ann, are you steamed at me?" I'm always in trouble and I'm not even that good a lay.

"We'll talk about it when we have more time. I have to do a bunch of stuff."

Back in the doghouse again. Three o'clock in the morning is usually when I get told exactly what's wrong with me. I finally fool myself to sleep around two-forty-five. At three o'clock, whatever woman I'm with elbows me and says, "I can't sleep." I ask her why and that's that for the next two hours.

I said, "What is it, Ann? Come on, tell me."

She was mad because I make plans with her only an hour ahead of time. All I know about why I do that is it's what I want to do. It's dumb, but it actually hurts me physically not to do what I want to do, or to do something I don't want to do. I'm spoiled maybe, although I try to be considerate. Sometime when I was a kid my emotions got crossed with physical pain. Asthma, gland trouble, hospitals, nerves, mood-swinging drugs, the typical things—that was my childhood. So what sanity I have, I have because to a great degree I try to do the easiest thing. It's moral too, I think. There's something moral about when your behavior is finally in sync with your nature.

Ann left the room, so I saw no reason I should continue the conversation. Women. You can't eat with 'em, you can't eat without 'em.

Mary graduated at the top of her class at Harvard, which impressed me because I was even held back in acting school. Mary was, I think, some third gender almost. At times her intelligence was so powerful it would kick her up into some place that was neither male nor female. When she got nervous at a dinner party or at an opening of some specialty bookstore that her college friends invited her to, she'd begin to talk a lot. Because of how porcelain and how lovely she was, people who didn't know her thought she was speeding or silly, at first. She'd talk about her cat, Entropy, to some stranger for an hour. These people were not in love with her, so they didn't necessarily give her the benefit of the doubt. She'd make a point though, she'd journey out there, miles from anything logical, and then tie it up to some interesting idea. I can't report exactly how it was, but occasionally she would dive into some overhead river of clarity about something. It didn't even seem as if she took any responsibility for it, but a person could get the "big picture" listening to her.

I climbed the three hundred floors to my dressing room to put on my policeman's uniform for the second act. Where was there to go? There was nowhere to go.

Ann wants a commitment. Why is it people only

use that word when referring to a mental hospital or a love affair?

Costumed and ready twelve hours in advance. I'm early for everything. My rhythms were off from the start. My mother has the same tendency. If we had to pick up my father at the airport, which we used to do regularly, we were painfully early.

"By the time we get to the airport, park, check the arrival time, it'll be time," my mother would say.

If my father's plane landed at four we'd be at the airport at noon. I'd be wheezing, and both me and my brother would be sloppy and irritable by twelve-fifteen. My mother would be fed up with us and angry and start a fight with my father the minute he stepped off the plane. All I ever wanted to do was grow up.

I made my entrance like a fool and was done for the night. Out on Seventh Avenue, it had gotten colder. All the shows were breaking so I had to go over to Sixth to get a cab. A woman cab driver picked me up. She had her dog on the front seat with her. I said, "The Broome Street Bar." She knew where it was. We didn't do any talking.

I was nervous. It was about ten-thirty. I'd be able to tell what Ansil looked like because of that night in the rain. And Mary had had some photographs of them together in her apartment. She'd also had one of me at her place too. I wondered if she had kept it out when he came over. There was a period when we both were seeing Mary at the same time.

I had the girl and her dog let me out on West Broadway so I could stall a little bit. But it was so cold I couldn't stand it. An old friend of mine from acting school, Johnny May, tends bar at the Broome Street. I was never really that close to him. He is a very good gambler and bookmaker. The acting teachers always owed him money.

I wanted a drink before I looked around the restaurant for Ansil.

"Sandy, how ya doin'?" Johnny May shouted at me.

I didn't want Ansil to see me before I at least had a whiskey or something.

"I'm freezing my balls off, Johnny May," I whispered. "You folks do a whiskey kind of thing here, or what?"

Johnny got me a shot. He then told me he had to go holler at a waitress. "If she orders a Greyhound she really means a Grasshopper. She's new. You gonna be here, Sandy? 'Cause let's bullshit."

I nodded. I gulped the drink down. Liquor never tastes good to me. I drink strictly to get drunk.

It didn't look like Ansil was there yet. It was a Monday and not crowded. I couldn't get Johnny May's attention for another drink. I got up to take my overcoat off and Ansil came in. He towered over me. He wasn't wearing an overcoat and his face and hands were pink from the cold. The girl who was seating people took us over to a quiet booth near a window in the restaurant section. Ansil ordered a whiskey and I ordered another one. He asked me if I had been waiting long and we got on how cold it was.

"I thought I could make it over here without a coat. I'm just down on Grand Street. But it's cold," he said.

There was some other talk like that and then drinks came, and we both started breathing for the first time.

"I'm glad you called me." I said. "Thank you."

He smiled and shook his head. He seemed like a WASP whose WASPness wasn't working for him the way it used to.

He said, "I pretty much told you all of it on the phone. You knew her. I don't know what else to say."

"Maybe there's nothing to say," I said.

We settled back in our seats and he looked out the window. A frozen bum was pushing an empty grocery cart.

"You're an actor?" he asked.

"Yeah."

"Mary told me. You're in a musical?"

"A comedy. I have a tiny part and I'm a standby. Mostly I do nothing but wait for somebody not to show up. That's my career."

"Uh-huh," he said and stared, looking straight at me and shaking his head three or four times too many. Then he looked down at his drink.

"You're a painter?" I asked.

"Huh?" He lifted his head and smiled kindly at me.

"You're an artist?"

"Usually I'm a sculptor. I'm working for some people who are reproducing certain famous pieces. Like Rodin's *Balzac* and Henry Moore's *Mother and Child*. In neon light," he said. He then shifted his position. He was too tall for the booth. "Cigarette?" He pulled a wrinkled pack of Camels out of his sweater.

"Thanks."

We lit up off the candle on the table. We were quiet for a while. Ansil stared back out the window and I looked around the restaurant. Across from us in a booth on the other side of the room a young, stylish girl was shaking her finger at a young man across from her. The young man shook his head wordlessly from side to side. The cigarette made me sick. I stubbed it out and took deep breaths to keep my stomach from backing up.

Ansil calmly said, "I don't think I've been to sleep in four days." He finished the last of his whiskey and waved the empty glass at the waitress going by. "You want another?" he asked me.

I nodded. "You'll get to sleep," I said. "It'll clobber you when it wants to."

Ansil pushed his fingers through his grey-speckled black hair and exhaled loudly. "I'm losing my mind."

The waitress brought another round. I wasn't even close to drunk.

"Maybe," I said, "maybe you're going to lose your mind for a while. And why the fuck shouldn't you?"

He took a gulp of his drink. "You know, I always used to think that I could stay on solid ground somehow. No matter what. But the first time you realize that that isn't necessarily true, you lose something, it's so terrifying. Am I being sufficiently vague?"

"Explain what you mean," I said.

"I never thought I could lose my mind, I guess. That a pain could be so intolerable I could lose my mind."

"A person," I said, "can get to the point where they're forced to say to themselves, It's in the pain's hands now. It's then a flip of the coin as to who remains after it's all over. You or the pain."

Ansil took another cigarette from the pack. "I'm gonna miss her."

"Yeah."

"Yeah," he said, and began to laugh. "That's what I've been trying to say."

We held our glasses up. "This is to her," I said.

"Right."

Ansil and I were both staring at the girl with the shaking finger in the booth across from us. She was very angry at the wimpy little guy across from her, just yapping and pointing at him. I tapped Ansil on the shoulder like David Niven would tap Errol Flynn in an RAF movie.

"What do you say, Ansil. Let's go over there and give her a sound thrashing."

He laughed in agreement.

"But first," I said, "we better have another drink. I think she has forty thousand pounds on us."

"You might be right."

"Tell you what, you buy this round," I said, "and then I'll offer to buy the other rounds. Then you say, no, Sandy, come on, this is my party. And then you buy all the other drinks after that."

We got the waitress's attention. As she smiled and twirled off I thought to myself: I have never wanted to bite anybody's ass so much in my life.

Ansil and I looked at each other and shared a smile and a nod. "Anybody Mary'd be with," I said, "can therefore virtually not be a scumbag. Am I right?"

Ansil tapped my hand. "You're right."

"Am I ever wrong?"

"I've never known you to be wrong."

The mean girl was still tearing into her guy across from us. She was getting more vocal now. We were getting some of the key statements.

"No! No! You don't. You don't feel that way, Mel. You say you do, but it's your behavior. It doesn't show up in your behavior."

"Ansil, could I ask, if you don't . . . if you can talk about it, you know, only if you can . . . would you tell me what was going on with her in the end?"

He gave out a little breath and shrugged.

"Just before she went to Boston she wanted to stay at her own apartment a lot more. Before that she'd been staying down at my place I'd say almost every night. It's bigger. It's a loft. I fixed up an area for her to do her writing in. But near the end—for no reason I could figure out—she wanted to spend a lot of nights back in her own place."

"And did she?"

He nodded.

"But the two of you were still together, right?" I asked.

The waitress set down our drinks. Ansil took a sip of his new whiskey.

"I thought it might be because she wanted to break up. But she swore it wasn't that, she told me she wanted to go back to her own place for a while, get things neat as a pin, she said, and spend a few nights there."

"And that's what she did?" I asked him.

"That's what she did. Then a few days later she went to Boston for her father's birthday."

"Hey, Sandy, you famous yet?"

It was my friend Johnny May.

"Not yet, Johnny May."

"Well, get famous so I can say I know you."

"Okay."

"Here's compliments of the house."

He put two more drinks down.

"Thanks a lot, Johnny." I introduced him to Ansil, then he went back to the bar.

I tried to think. Why did Mary swallow pills that would make her dead? It might have been too many painful people and things. It is just luck that everybody doesn't do it. It's probably just luck that keeps obstacles surmountable.

"I feel she was really going off there near the end," Ansil said. "I don't know what anyone could have done to have helped."

"What do you mean?"

"She was sick. She was getting sicker all the time I knew her."

"Yeah," I said. "I guess she just—"

He wasn't looking at me, but in a sudden movement that kind of scared me, he brought his big head close to mine, staring straight down at the table.

"One time she came home late from work, you know"—his eyes caught mine for a split second—"we were watching some movie on television and I looked over at her and I saw that she was jabbing a pushpin in and out of her leg."

"Jesus!"

"There was a thin stripe of blood going down her leg. She didn't even know she was doing it. When I yelled at her and pointed at the blood, she looked so ashamed."

"What did you do?"

"I tried to make light of it in a way. I called her psychiatrist in the morning, to tell him. This German guy. He was a real stereotype, Vornow is his name. Anyway, all he said to me was, 'Call the instant she does anything like that again.' "

"Good solid advice," I said. "The Nazi prick!"

"I had met him once or twice," Ansil went on, "when I'd take her up to her appointments. I tried to get her to change doctors because I believed he was in love with her. This was her *psychiatrist*."

"You really believe he loved her?" I asked him. I was drunk now and my mouth was wide open.

"Yes, I seriously do."

Ansil was bright red now in his anger at the doctor.

"What makes you think so?"

"By the way he didn't look at me."

"Nazi," I said. "The Allies should have kept marching. What do you say," I said too loudly, "should we get even more shit-faced drunk, or what?"

Ansil settled into thinking about something he seemed far from ready to talk about. After two and a half silent drinks for Ansil, and one and a half more for me, we were both on planet Q. Ansil tried to light the same cigarette several times with a wet match.

"You know," he finally said to me, shaking his head, "God should go up for reelection. He's had the job long enough."

"Absolutely right. Too old for the gig." I was in a daze by then and hoped what I said answered what Ansil said.

"Exactly," replied Ansil. Then he said, "God may be a woman."

"You think so?" I said.

"It's possible," he replied. "This whole women's movement and everything." He offered me his last unlit cigarette and a wet match.

"Yeah," I said. "Built-in block of votes there. Of course as soon as a female God gets into office, men can kiss even safe sex good-bye."

"You think?"

"Stands to reason," I explained, "because then not only will women have the power of their looks, which I'm sure you'll agree, Ansil, is substantial—"

"Substantial. Go on."

"But then they'll . . . what the fuck . . . where was I?"

"You were—"

"Oh, yeah. Just that the deck is gonna be stacked and so are the women. Ha ha ha. But then that's gonna be it. We still have a little work to do on our theory. I've got the good folks up at Duke University smoothing out the inconsistencies for me."

"Good," Ansil said. "If you're not gonna want that cigarette. . . ."

"Yeah, you take it and not smoke it for a while. I'm trying to give up holding it in my mouth and not being able to light it."

As it got empty around us I tried to see how much undrunkenness was left in me to get home on. After a pause that could have lasted longer or shorter than it seemed, Ansil and I agreed we'd attempt to stand up and leave.

Getting my overcoat on, I was like Houdini struggling out of chains. I fell over completely after one sleeve. We finally made it to the door. It was snowing when we got outside, and I stuck my tongue up to meet the flakes.

The snow had warmed up the weather. We stood in front of the Broome Street Bar. Ansil was staring straight ahead. He shook his head up and down, slowly, as if he were agreeing with someone. I guess I was looking for a cab. I don't know what I was doing. I moved back and forth from a strange anger to drunkenness. I didn't want to go home and sit in my bathtub and read until I could sleep. I wanted a new girl but I wasn't famous enough to make it easy to get one at that hour. I wanted to go home and have my "Father Knows Best" wife waiting up for me. I wish I had never seen a movie or a television show. I wondered who I'd be then.

"You know, Ansil, we need a drink. Because here's why. The night is three drinks ahead of us. What do you think?"

"Yes."

"Yeah. Let's go back in, sit at the bar, look at the waitress's ass. Somehow life's whole gestalt is in waitresses' asses. Anyway, I should go back to say good-bye to the bartender. I went to school with him and I should say good night. Because, Ansil, as my father said, it's important to be nice to people because you never know when you can use them."

We turned around and went back inside. I took

my overcoat off and we hollered our choice of beverage to Johnny May.

"Hey," Johnny May said. "You look like two guys who just left here."

"I had to come back in, Johnny. I wanted my friend Ansil here to have one more drink. He's going into the service tonight."

"How you doing, Ansil?" Johnny May wiped off his big, wet hand on his apron and stuck it over the bar at Ansil.

"Yeah," I continued, "he's going into the USO. He's taking a production of *Look Back in Anger* to a GI weather station in Iceland. Those boys are starved for realistic drama up there. I swear to God if they have to sit through one more performance of *Bajour* I don't know what they'll do."

Johnny May had stopped listening to me three hours ago. Ansil was downing his drink through a smile that looked like a face-lift.

"Damn." I slapped the bar counter. "Why didn't I think of this earlier? We need some dames down here. I'm gonna call this girl I'm semiseeing and get her down here. We'll listen to some girl-talk for a while. What do you think, Ansilonia?"

He shrugged like he didn't really want to. But I wanted to a lot.

"Come on." I put my arm around him. "We'll stay up late, we'll do each other's hair. It's not that late and it can't get any darker."

A craving comes over me sometimes. Often, actually. I need a female around me to show off for or something. For several uncomplex reasons, I like to look at them and have them be there when I'm drunk. The excitement of their proximity helps me to say smarter and funnier things because I want them. I used to want them and didn't even care what I was saying. But now, even if I don't get them, the presence of women is a drug. It helps me put words and jokes to what has been driving me crazy.

I was at the pay phone trying to call Ann. I don't know how late it was, but through the open kitchen door of the restaurant I could see the Puerto Rican chef putting on his overcoat. I took the phone from its cradle and cracked it against my forehead looking for my ear. I got the quarter into the slot and dialed extra carefully.

Three or four rings and Ann answered with a voice that had that midsleep mucus in it. "Hi ya, honey," I said cheerfully. "Christ, I woke ya. I'm sorry. I didn't think it was so late. I'll hang up. You want me to hang up?"

"Huh, who is it?" she said, her voice not in control yet.

"It's Sandy. I'm sorry, honey. Go back to sleep."

"Oh, that's okay, Sandy. Where are you? Hold it, let me turn the light on. Where are you, Sandy?"

Ansil had come over to the booth and was handing me a drink.

"Honey, I'm a little drunk. I'm with my friend Ansil and we're having a great time. You should come down here with us and be with us and everything."

Ansil looked at his watch, which he wore with the face hiply displayed on the inside of his wrist.

"Maybe if you want," she said, "you and your friend . . ."

"Ansil," I reminded her.

". . . I'll fix you something to eat. If you want there's things to drink here. You want to come up?"

I called Ansil back toward the phone. He had wandered over to where the great waitress was counting her tips.

"Ansil, let's go up to Ann's! She's gonna make us

some food and we'll have some drinks up there. What do ya say?"

He shook his head. "You go ahead. I don't know her and it's late and—"

"Do you have to get up early tomorrow or what?"

"No, but I don't know—"

"Come on," I insisted. "We'll have some laughs. She's a good girl. We'll eat something. She'll make us something great. She's nuts like that. She really will make something. She'll *prepare* something. She's a major cook."

I was pushing. I was pushing Ansil and Ann. I wanted him to come with me. I wanted her to get up and have us there. I was getting a little cracked. Sometimes late nights made me nuts and bad blood boils up in me. If I had to come out with some of the truth of how I was feeling, it was, fuck you, Ansil. Fuck you for having more of a hold on Mary than I did. No matter how much I got out of the relationship. And fuck you for your stupid name, Ansil. What kind of a name is that? And fuck Ann for liking me too. Because doesn't anybody know that I'm crazy and have two or more people inside me? And why do I have to feel that I should work at being happy? And why haven't I ever learned anything the easy way? And I also thought, fuck Mary, if it came to that. And fuck God if he calls me up in front of him and says I was a shit to use people, because if he catches me in the right mood I might spit in his eye and say, I'll explain myself after you explain to me how you let even babies die.

I was drunk and had to make Ansil come with me. Maybe it was because if Mary loved him too there was something of me in him, and then maybe I'd be able to see what it was. Because as it was I looked into every mirror I walked by and I hadn't seen myself in one yet.

Ansil shrugged and smiled. He would come.

"Annie, we're coming up. You sure it's okay? We'll be up. We'll take a cab."

I got my coat on again and headed outside. We found a cab a block into the night. The driver was an Israeli. I told Ansil I was getting very hungry and what a good idea it was that we had stretched out the night. But it wasn't a good idea. It was a weird idea. I was making it happen anyway.

Ann was a talented costume designer, although she only repaired another costume designer's costumes for the crap show we worked for. I'd seen pictures of some of the things she made for the productions of the college she went to in Connecticut. She has imagination, and she takes her work seriously.

I know a guy, Seth I'll call him, although his name is closer to Bart. Seth is an alcoholic. His mother left him a little money when she died, so he bought a bar on University Place. Now he drinks with friends and strangers at his own place. Although he's only forty or so—and he'd be the first to tell you this—he's not long for this world. But he wants to drink himself to death in sort of a sacred way. "I can't stop, but I don't want to be one of those crumbs down on the Bowery rubbing the grime off people's windshields for fifteen cents at the red light." He bows to the formidable nature of his addiction, so has placed it in a context of his choice. No matter how bad it may be that he's killing himself, he's making something blackly artistic out of it. Other arts don't kill you as fast, but Seth's not that lucky. Or he might be, depending on how you feel at the moment.

Ann made costumes well. She studied all about them and her job had a place of real respect in her life. When you meet people who take the right things seriously you always feel that they may have the right slant on one or two other things as well. Of course, we all have the adult-strength loneliness. And how do I know I'm not dreaming anyway?

Ann made Ansil and me stand by the fire to warm up while she poured brandies for us. She had on her robe with all the Monet paint colors in it. I was her Wayward Boy and Company. Ansil was polite and quietly drunk. He looked at her ballet books on the shelf and the Beatrix Potter dolls that sat beside them. I followed Ann into the kitchen and started the apology business up again.

"It's fine," she said. "I'm glad you came up, Sandy."

There was no reason for anyone but Ann to be there. I didn't know why I talked Ansil into coming uptown with me. I knew less about why he agreed. I wasn't in love with Ann. I'm not saying I should have been, but—and this is the strange part—I got to thinking that in order to keep on doing the kinds of things we did together I should either feel more for her, or not mind that I didn't feel enough. Waking up on Sunday mornings and eating a great breakfast she'd say she would have made anyway, or lounging around together and listening to a symphony while we traded off pages of the *Times* made me feel as if I could do it all over again next week and not feel any more for her. Whereas I felt she was feeling more for me, even if she said she wasn't.

Ansil said he was really tired and that maybe he'd go home, so I said, "Do some yoga and wake the hell up."

Ann put on a recording of Liszt piano music.

"Ummm, pretty," Ansil said.

"Liszt," said Ann.

"Who's playing?" he asked her.

"Aldo Ciccolini," she replied.

And then there was a pause in which nobody asked anybody anything.

"Yes," I volunteered. "Aldo Ciccolini, the least known and least understood Marx brother." No laugh.

Ansil was on the floor in front of the stereo with the album cover up over his eyes. And I thought he was thinking of leaving, didn't you?

"Annie," I tapped her on the shoulder. She was facing one of her hanging plants, rubbing one of its leaves and shaking her head. "Annie, do you have any grass left from the other night?"

"In the jar by the bed. You know where it is," she said without taking her eyes off the plant, which I guessed was dying. I don't have any plants in my apartment. I'm not getting my ass up at six A.M. and walking them out in the cold winter snow. Not me. Not this citizen.

I was sitting on Ann's big bed, rolling the biggest joint any white man has ever seen and listening to Ansil and Ann.

Ann said, "Sandy hasn't mentioned you. Do you know each other long?"

"We met tonight. It's a strange story."

I interrupted and shouted into the other room, "He grabbed my dick in the Times Square shuttle."

I lit the joint. I don't smoke too much of anything because a doctor once told me I had emphysemic lungs. I had severe asthma as a child, so as a bonus my parents moved us to Miami which is always hot and always humid and where there has never once been any air. Two minutes after I'd leave our frozen air-conditioned house my shirt would be sticking to my back from the sweat and my breathing would be shallow or nonexistent. There was also nothing good to look at in Miami and no one worth knowing.

Ann came into the bedroom and I handed her the joint. "Sandy, come into the other room. What are you doing in here all by yourself?"

"Just daydreaming. Hey, Ann, you pissed off at me or what?"

"No, nothing's wrong. Come on into the other room, Sandy."

Ansil was slapping his hands on his pockets looking for a cigarette.

"Here, kid." I took the joint from Ann and handed it to him. "Smoke this and be somebody."

I stood by the window, watching snow fall in white bedsheets to the ground.

"It's snowing out, but don't come over here to look at it," I said. "It's personal."

Ann put another one of those phoney cancer logs on the fire and replaced the lamp with a candle.

"I think I prefer to freeze to death if I get a choice," I said.

Ansil said, "That's the best way to go." And then he looked over at Ann and shook his head as if to convince her he wasn't kidding, that they do indeed say that it's the best way to go.

Ann had brought out some neatly cut chunks of cheese on a wooden plank and put it on the floor between her and Ansil.

"You know," I said as I lay down on the couch behind them, "you two wonderful kids should get married and live out in Bucks County and have a family and rent me an apartment over the barn. I'd come up for weekends 'cause that's, I think, what it is I am. Or should be. A very nice uncle."

"Sandy," Ann said and slapped at the cuff of my pants with the cheese knife, "you know you want to have kids."

"No, I don't. I don't know that. Not without a million dollars. Or not unless they're my wife's kids from another marriage and they spend their weekends with their biological father. Ansil has a kid, he'll tell ya."

Ansil smiled with half his mouth and reassured Ann that he did not really have a kid. Then he gave her a smile that had a "You know Sandy" in it.

Ann handed the two of us cocktail napkins and asked how we knew each other.

"We had a mutual friend," I answered. "I told you, didn't I, Ann, about Mary?" I poured myself and Ansil some more brandy although his glass didn't need it as badly as mine did.

"Ann, you wouldn't have any cigarettes around?" Ansil asked.

"I keep some around for my friends who smoke. I have menthol and not. Which?"

"Not."

She went to get the cigarettes, saying without turning around, "Oh, you know Mary too, Ansil?"

There was a pause, and then I figured I'd put an end to the show.

"She passed away, Ann. Mary passed away. Ansil was her boyfriend."

What was I gonna say so that it didn't sound like it did? Ann stopped pulling out a drawer in midpull.

"Oh, my God, I'm sorry, Ansil."

She didn't say "Oh, my God" as dramatically as it could have been said. But she didn't do a bad job with it either. I may have misread it, or maybe I've gotten to a point where I think people are as bad as I am, but I thought I saw Ansil shifting his expression to where it would do him the most good with Ann.

And where was Mary in all of this? And where was she in my gladness of me not being her? Jesus Christ! The glove life puts on your heart.

Some sexual madmen dismember the women they rape. They are insanely determined to pare away the mystery of why their victims' beauty controls and torments them so. Do they then discover that the mystery is too huge to be housed in someone's body? And isn't the beauty of this life just as vast and horrible?

Ansil lit up the stale cigarette Ann gave him. She gave me the grass to roll and asked if we were hungry. Ansil raised an eyebrow yes.

"I'm always hungry," I answered. "Always and constantly hungry, until I eat. And then I'm totally unhappy that I ate because I don't want to get fat and then two hours later I'm hungry again and the whole ugly rotten process that is my life begins anew. You know what I'm saying?" I said.

Ann wanted to know if omelets were okay. They were "wonderful" with Ansil.

"Sandy, how about you?" she asked and sat down next to me and took hold of my two ears, which resemble two large old velvet suits hanging off the sides of my head.

"Sounds great, honey. With bacon?" I asked.

"Sure with bacon," she said.

"I'm a happy woman," I yelled as she left us for the kitchen.

I gulped some brandy and started to roll another unnecessary joint.

"She's really nice, Sandy," Ansil said.

"Yes, she is. She's a good girl." I offered him some more brandy.

"No thanks."

"How are you feeling? You feeling okay, Ansil?"

"Fine."

"You know," I said, "remember when Mary was working for that mean scumbag of a publisher up on Fifty-seventh Street?"

"Helen?"

"Yeah, Helen something. And Mary finally quit after this woman had been treating her like shit for months?"

"That woman was sick."

"Yeah. She quit working for her just after she and you—well, when she stopped seeing me." I stopped to light the joint. I took a deep drag and held it. I exhaled and kept the joint in my mouth. "Anyway, I ran into Mary on Fifty-seventh Street after that and, you know Mary, she was always complaining about how that woman worked her like a slave."

"It's true, though," Ansil said. "She did treat her that way. And Mary would always take it. She let people do that to her all the time."

"Yeah. I know," I said. "But then she told me that this nobody wouldn't pay her some money she owed her. And do you know, Ansil, right there on Fifty-seventh Street I felt like going up to that woman Helen's office, and do you know what I thought I'd do? I thought I'd lock me and her in her office and hold her typewriter out the window until she came up with Mary's dough."

Ansil laughed and asked me why I hadn't done it.

"Because you should have done it," I said.

I waited a second, then laid the joint down on the ashtray between us. We looked at each other and then I went into the kitchen. Ann was taking the eggs off the stove when we heard the front door open and close.

That night I had a dream that I hitched a ride on a rocket about to blast off from Cape Canaveral. I arranged with the astronaut to drop me off at the planet where Mary lived now that she was dead and pick me up on his way back.

"Okay," the astronaut said, "but don't be late or we'll miss the window in space that allows us to get home."

I told him I wouldn't be late. When he dropped me off on Mary's planet she was right there to meet me. "I just have a couple of minutes, Mary," I told her. "I just came to ask you something."

"What is it?" she asked taking my hand.

"Was I a good enough friend to you?"

"You're here, aren't you?" she answered.

Then in my dream Mary took a black wedding ring made of elephant hair off her finger and put it on mine. The rocket came to take me back.

TUESDAY

The next morning Ann got up early to go to dance class. She left coffee and a note telling me I could sleep as late as I wanted and to drop her key off in the mailbox when I left.

I'd told her that Ansil had left the way he did because the Mary thing had him all busted up.

I lay there listening to Third Avenue scream up at me, telling myself I was still asleep. I opened my left eye and saw the empty brandy glass on the bed table. I wasn't going to live very long, that was for sure. My head pounded in a Euro-Disco beat, and my mouth was kicking me in the ass. I was immediately remorseful about everything in general.

I guess I pulled something on Ansil and I guess I felt guilty about it but I said, "Fuck him," out loud anyway. I got out of bed and headed for the kitchen. I heated up some coffee and looked at my hung-over self in the mirror over the sink. Neither of me liked what we saw. Ann had left an English muffin in the Toast-R-Oven. I plugged it in and began toast-R-ing.

I went back into the living room and put Arthur Rubinstein's recording of Saint-Saëns' Concerto in G on the stereo. The coffee's speed was settling my stomach. In the kitchen the muffin still wasn't ready, but I buttered and ate it anyway. I brought my coffee into the bathroom, where there was a huge photograph of Baryshnikov next to the toilet. He probably never gets drunk. He's great looking and not only that, he's the star ballet dancer of the world *and* he's straight. A straight ballet dancer. And he looks like that. I think maybe he's gotten some trim in his life. What do you think?

I looked at myself in the bathroom mirror for a while then wrapped myself in a big towel and went back to the living room. I was listening to music and sitting by the window watching the people in the office building across the street when I started thinking about the day I met Mary.

I had been at a photocopying place on Bleecker Street in the West Village. I had been there earlier in the day to pick up some acting résumés. I didn't bother to look at what kind of job they did until I got home, an hour later. Then I saw that they had blurred my last name. I went back to the place. When I got there a young woman was just handing in something to be copied. It was Mary. I remember the guy was rushing her, even though I was the only other person in line.

"Yes, miss, you told me you want three copies of each."

"No," Mary told the guy very nicely. "I want five copies of each. You weren't listening."

"You said three copies. But I'll give you five copies if you want them."

The guy was being unnecessarily nasty and I was in such a foul mood that I opened my mouth.

"Excuse me, sir," I said. "The lady did say five copies, you know. Five copies, she said. So why don't you just give them to her without the cross-examination?"

Actually I hadn't heard Mary say anything. The guy acted like he didn't want to waste his valuable time answering me and gave Mary her receipt. She moved away from the counter and I gave him the résumés and said that I needed them done "in such a way that you can read my last name."

Then I heard Mary laughing behind me. I turned and took my first look at her. I held up one of the résumés for her to see. "I got a Rorschach test for a last name here." She smiled. Seeing her face for the first time was like seeing New York for the first time. It thrilled and made you feel like you lived there, that you had been out of town and were finally home.

The guy took the résumés out of my hand. I looked back at him. He said he'd do them over, I thanked him nicely, and he gave me another receipt and told me I could pick the job up in a couple of hours. I'd heard the bell on the front door of the place ring while the guy was writing up my receipt and I thought it was just someone coming in. But it had been Mary going out. I wanted to catch up to her so I hurried out. But I didn't see her anywhere. She had disappeared so quickly it was almost spooky. I looked all over for her and even moved out into the middle of Bleecker Street to get a better overall view, but she wasn't anywhere. And then from behind me I heard her call my name. She was coming out of the health food store right next to the copying place. She had a little brown bag in her hand and I took in for the first time everything she was wearing: khaki shorts, knee socks, sandals, crisp navy blue shirt, a pink sweater, and a straw hat with a purple band. If she had had that hat on when I first looked at her I didn't notice.

"What are you doing in the middle of the street, Sandy Inkspot?"

"Well, I figured since I couldn't find you I'd just wait here for a gypsy cab to run me down."

She laughed and held up her paper bag.

"Would you like some apple juice?"

Would I? I walked toward her and some idiot on a bike, in those stupid tight racing shorts, almost killed me.

When I got to the sidewalk she thanked me for standing up to the guy behind the counter for her. I asked what her name was. She told me. I remember having all the feelings I usually have when I meet someone beautiful. Except that I wasn't nervous. Because of something Mary gave off, like a perfume. And I could tell she liked me. I told her my real last name. She thought Bayard was interesting. I suggested we take a stroll over to Abingdon Square Park. When we got to the street just before the park I took Mary's arm. It was a totally instinctive thing. It wasn't at all like you take other women's arms—you know, just to get the touching started. No. Mary's arm you took to make sure she got across the street.

It was about twelve-thirty on a summer afternoon. It was a weekday and beautiful. When we got to the bench I asked Mary what she was having copied. She told me it was a story she had written.

"It's about a couple, a man and a woman and a

woman friend of theirs. And the couple turn their back on the woman when she leaves a man the couple likes. The woman was a friend of the couple's years before she introduced them to the man, you see. So when the couple turn their back on her she feels so betrayed she can hardly get over it."

"That sounds really interesting," I said. "What's it called?"

"'The Turn of the Century.'"

I laughed. And I thought, who *is* this girl? She opened up the apple juice and offered me some, apologizing for not having any cups.

"Oh," I said, "we don't need any."

Then she said, "Yeah, it's like two young people going to a lake at midnight."

"What do you mean?"

"You know," she said. "The girl says to the boy, 'We don't have any swimsuits.' And the boy says back, 'We don't need any.'"

I remember we just sat on that bench for a long time. She told me she had the day off from work in the script department of some soap opera and how wonderful it was for her not to have to get up at five-thirty in the morning. She held her straw hat on with one hand and lifted the bottle of juice to her mouth with the other. I was in love with her.

"What kind of acting do you do, Sandy?" She knew I was an actor from having seen my résumé.

"Forced."

She pushed me and I fell off the bench. It was one of the few times in my life I ever wanted to talk about someone other than myself. "What about you, Mary? You're a writer, huh? You sure have eyes like a writer, whatever it is I mean by that."

"Well, I'm not published or anything. I write a lot of poetry. Although now I've started to write stories."

"Tell me about one, okay?"

"Well"—she took a deep breath and began like she was a little girl in front of the class—"now I'm writing a story about a teenage boy who takes his retarded older brother to a Yankees game. The retarded boy knows everything about baseball, especially the Yankees. There are two pretty young girls in front of the two brothers. And the four of them strike up a conversation and almost catch a foul tip from Willie Randolph."

We talked some more about a lot of things and then walked over to the docks to look at New Jersey. I did a lot of Herman Melville whaling shtick on the pier, which she laughed at. She made me laugh too.

"Hey, Mary, where'd you get them purple eyes?" I asked her.

"Well"—deep breath—"one night my father called me and my brother Jake into the living room and asked which one of us wanted the purple eyes."

"Yeah . . ."

"And I raised my hand first."

I laughed for a while about that.

In no time she told me about her mother running off a few weeks before her twelfth birthday and about her father being a very well-known doctor who was famous for inventing a new treatment for diabetes. After that she told me she'd been in a mental institution. She said the main reason had been because she was exhausted and run down, having worked by day as a college student and at night as a waitress. Her well-to-do father wanted her to help pay for her Harvard education.

I had trouble believing her when she told me all those dramatic things. For one thing, I had just met her. But mostly I had trouble believing her because if any of those things had happened to me, with my iron constitution, I most likely would have wound up chained to an oak tree behind the workhouse with saliva shooting out of my mouth. It was also hard to believe because things like that should be hard to believe. Mothers shouldn't run off a few days before their kids' twelfth birthdays, and rich fathers with obviously frail daughters should give them a few lousy bucks to eat on.

It began to cloud up. Mary invited me back to her place for a glass of wine. Her apartment was tiny. She had a portable, non–electric typewriter with a large stack of poems next to it. There were some black-and-white drawings on the walls. Her Harvard diploma hung over the kitchen sink. I saw a couple of pictures of Ansil around the place. Of course, I didn't know it was Ansil at the time. I simply thought he was just another better-looking guy. Entropy, her cat, made me sneeze.

"Are you allergic to cats?"

"No. Whenever it starts to rain I sneeze."

There was a special little shelf off in a hard-to-notice corner with a trophy and a couple of brass and colored-ribbon medals on it.

"What's this?" I asked, moving uninvited toward them.

"I was on the swimming team in college."

I turned to watch her pull her sweater up over her head. She was slight and fine.

I told her that a lot of woman swimmers are built like Robert Mitchum.

She laughed hard then told me, without kidding, that she'd found a way to turn in the water so as not to get too big. That spooked me a little.

We drank a lot of wine and talked, recognizing each other's experiences. High in the best way wine can make you, I kissed her and she kissed me back just as fully, but with a message in it that we weren't going to make love then. I was just as happy. Not in a perv way, I started to take off my pants anyway. Maybe it wasn't innocent. I wanted her. But we were drunk enough to recognize that I wasn't taking my pants off the way a fifty-eight-year-old guy does behind his secretary's back.

We kissed deeply, my hand touching the electric part of her nipple, our hearts twice their normal temperature, but we weren't going to make love. Mary shook her head, looked down at my pants twisted around one of my legs and laughed. It was okay. We weren't embarrassed by my behavior. I started leering at her like I was a schoolyard flasher and she, laughing a large, almost manlike laugh, rolled up the *New York Times Magazine* and beat me over the head with it, out the door. I was really laughing too.

"Take me to see *Rocky* tomorrow night, Sandy Bayard," she said as I left.

"You never saw it?" I asked.

"Nope."

The next night I took her to a revival house. She touched my hand at the part where Rocky forgives Burgess Meredith for taking his locker away and lets Meredith be his manager.

Later that night, not drunk, and after sharing a Monte Cristo sandwich at Rumpelmayer's, we made love back at her place.

All the broken bones in her heart, all the frailty got washed out. Not because of anything about me, except maybe I liked her so much. We were sexy and timely and strong with each other, and she was being this other person that she could be.

My coffee had gotten cold. I put the cup in the sink and went back into Ann's bedroom to get dressed. As I was putting my watch on I suddenly remembered I had a commercial audition scheduled that morning. I was already late. I didn't even have time to shower or go downtown to my place and change. I used Ann's deodorant and dragged her leg razor over my face a couple of times, continually cutting myself. I rushed out of her apartment and got into a cab driven by an angry old man named Milton Gomms.

As usual the casting people were running behind schedule so I hadn't missed anything. The audition was for a Burger King commercial, and I was up for the role of the Burger King himself, so you can imagine how nervous I was. The director kept screaming things at me like, "No, no, no. You can't say 'burger-licious' like that. You have to say it in a more regal way." But I couldn't. I couldn't say it in a more regal way.

Anyway, I finally got back to my place around noon. Mrs. Floyd, my landlady, stopped me just outside my building.

"Sandy, the berler is broke again. No hot water. The Puerto Rican kid was supposed to come. I been waiting all morning for him but he's not here yet."

Mrs. Floyd used to be fat and jolly. One New Year's Eve when I had just moved into the building she and her husband invited me in to drink rum punch with them and watch Guy Lombardo. Mr. Floyd was always crocked and an inch away from tears at all times. They had two sons, Dennis and Junior, both of them firemen. Junior had died in the line of duty and Dennis had contracted a non–job-related eye disease and was living on his fireman's insurance in Canarsie with his nineteen-year-old wife and her son from a previous marriage to another deceased fireman. A few years back Mr. Floyd disappeared. Mrs. Floyd got very skinny. I came back from doing a play one summer in Stockbridge, Massachusetts, and saw her sweeping the front stoop. The front of her had caved in. Now she's always knocking on my door asking me to unscrew jars of mayonnaise for her.

"There's never any fucking hot water in the fucking winter time!" I mumbled to myself as I was getting my mail out of the box. It was just one letter, a flyer for Pilar's play. I locked my mailbox, turned to let myself into the building, and there, resting on the grill that borders the stained glass window of the building's front door, was a letter from Mary, "This was in my box" penciled across it.

I could hardly get my key in the entrance door. I went up to my place, put the letter down in the living room, went back, locked the door behind me, hung up my overcoat, took off my shoes, went back into the living room, picked up the letter, and looked at her name and return address again. The envelope appeared to have been folded up a few times and had come open in the back and had been taped closed.

I opened it. It was just one quarter of a sheet of lined paper with this written diagonally across the page: *"It's nothing you've done, but it feels like it is."* And that was it. Two lines.

My head spun around inside my collar, like in *The Exorcist*. I put the letter down and paced the room. Thank you very much. I was frightened. What was this supposed to mean, *It's nothing you've done, but it feels like it is*. Give me a break. "I didn't do anything," I said out loud.

I started the bath water running and then remembered there was no hot water, so I went over to the stereo and put on the classical music radio station instead. I got a low-tar cigarette from the pack I keep around in case I get a letter from the dead. My stomach felt like a lobster was pinching it.

That love affair was just like I remember it. I don't have anything to be scared about, I thought.

I poured myself a huge glass of Bolla wine and read the letter again. Then I picked up the phone and called my friend Henry Davis. Henry is an eighty-year-old psychologist. About six years before, I started seeing him because I was close to a nervous breakdown. I had broken up with someone and was a mess. A psychic I went to see as a last resort told me, "You act like you're crazy. Go see my friend Henry Davis and he'll help you straighten yourself out."

Well, I did go to see him and I was all right. It truly had taken me years to believe it. But of course, now I was thinking that I was totally cracked again. That all my progress was just an illusion.

Whenever I called Henry and said "Hi!" he always said, "Hello, Sandy," like he fully expected it to be me when the phone rang. I told him that it was urgent that I see him, as I thought I was going a little nuts. Actually what I said was that I was real scared about something. He told me to come right over.

He lived near Chinatown in a beautiful little brownstone apartment.

The girl I couldn't get over when I went to see Henry was the first and only woman I ever lived with. Her name was Rebecca, and probably still is. She was very beautiful and American looking. I think some of her relatives are still coming over on the *Mayflower*. We were both twenty-one and she'd already been married for two years and separated. She moved in with me at the end of our second date. I was in love with the whole idea of her and the idea of living with someone just like the friends I looked up to lived with. Someone just like the guy I wanted to be would live with. She had that skin with the permanent tan and sexy buckteeth. "Trombone Teeth," I called her.

The relationship was over in eight months. I drove her completely crazy. She left me for a carpenter. I was even jealous of men she hadn't met yet. But making love with Rebecca was the first time I got the idea of what sex could be like. We were junkies for each other.

We fucked and tasted and held each other like it would be suicide to let go. The chemistry was strong. We barely made it home with our clothes on. We once found a way to make love in the Hayden Planetarium on a crowded Sunday afternoon without being caught and tossed into pervert jail. We had our problems though and weren't even close to being as mature as we thought we were. If you have an affair that passionate when you're older you might wake up one morning with an ambulance driver sitting on your chest attaching you to jumper cables.

As I said, Henry Davis was in his early seventies when I first met him. He was taller than I was—about six-foot-two. He had close-cropped hair. He wore then, and pretty much always wore, a navy blue velour pull-over shirt and khaki pants.

The first day I met him his wife, Jane, opened the door. She was a very pretty woman in her late sixties and the author of popular children's books. She and Henry had no children. Henry said that they decided there were "plenty of children without ours." He was a certified psychologist and had been a student of Alfred Adler's. In their early life together, Henry and Jane had worked exclusively with alcoholics and "other egomaniacs" as he called them. And in the fifties they had run a school for retarded children. "There are no retarded children," Henry once said to me, "just over-competitive families."

I was extremely nervous when I first met him—smoking cigarettes and unable to sit still. But I knew I needed help. The end of my relationship with Rebecca was the brick wall that my speeding-out-of-control life had smashed into. A terrible jealousy erupted in me when I thought of her with another man. It was when we were no longer together that it drove me the craziest. It was true, of course, that I definitely didn't want to actually be with her anymore. She wasn't someone whose company I actually enjoyed. We didn't much like each other or get along. But I loved having her with me in a group of my friends. I especially liked it when she put her arm around me at the correct moments in public. But to be alone with her wasn't good, except for the sex. But even the sex near the end of it had become a form of insurance against loss, trying to do it right so as to be guaranteed one more day. Because if I lost her she'd find somebody else.

I remember hoping that Rebecca would magically die. Die suddenly and tragically, painlessly too. I wasn't a total monster. If she'd just die. The hero I would have been then. But old lovers never die, they just show up a year later at somebody's party with a better-looking date than yours.

Anyway, during that first session with Henry I was describing, very dramatically, the pain I felt when I thought of Rebecca in the arms of "some other man" when Henry interrupted me. "Why'd you pick someone you were going to be jealous with? What did you think you were after?"

"I wasn't after anything," I said. "We had this terribly strong love and—"

"Were you jealous a lot when the two of you were still together?"

"Just the last four months or so."

"How long were you together?"

"Eight months."

"Uh-huh," he said. "Well, if you had this terribly strong love, why should you care what she did. Why did you care who she rolled in the hay with as long as he wasn't on top of her when you wanted to be?"

I was outraged. I couldn't believe this old scuzz was talking to me like this. And he went on. "Pretty hostile stuff, you know. Manipulating people to do what you want just so you won't be jealous. Who are you? The King of England or something?"

"Look, I love Rebecca and—"

"That's a crock. You don't love her. You hate her guts."

"I hate her guts?" I was really outraged now.

"And even if you could control your desire to control her, the fact that you can control yourself doesn't add up to much anyway. Because if you have to control yourself so much, you picked the wrong woman to begin with."

"You know, I don't think I hate Rebecca. I mean, I really don't think I do, I'm just so crazy, I'm just so crazy."

"You're not crazy. You're just too attached to people. There aren't any good attachments."

"I don't know what you mean about no good attachments, because I'd like to get married some day. You're married."

He shook his head and said, "How're you gonna have a relationship when you want the world to have a plot like a movie? You have to unstick yourself from other people, and then you'll find out who you are. Find out what you really like so you can choose a companion you're comfortable with. Someone you don't have to work at it with so hard. The other person is supposed to try to make things easier. If it's so hard you're doing it wrong. Unstick yourself. We're alone in this world, and that fact can either depress you or set you free."

I didn't know what the hell he was talking about for the most part. But I desperately needed another way of looking at things. Another way might release me from the grip of other people's opinions, a grip I let them get on me in the first place. It was as if someone had turned the air conditioner on in a very hot room.

A room I had never left before or had known existed. The psychic was right. Henry helped me, right from the start. After a while I felt better. Feeling better was the proof I needed.

When I asked Henry how much I owed him he said, "Can you afford thirty dollars?" He never let me pay him anything at all after that first meeting. "Where I'm going I won't be needing any money," he said.

I got to Henry's by cab fifteen minutes after I called him. I had Mary's letter in my pocket. I hadn't seen Henry for about eight months. He looked very tired. His eyes were dark and watery.

"Hi, Henry, thanks a lot for seeing me so quickly, it's just—"

"Bayard, you keepin' out of trouble?"

"Been tryin', Henry. I got this—"

He disappeared into the kitchen and said something I couldn't make out. I stood in the hall looking at one of the new paintings he had done. His paintings are nuts. They are usually of faceless, round-headed people running through streets or watering flowers that blossom into the same round-headed people. A lot of his pictures have his own language or words written on them in letters that look Japanese but aren't.

"What'd you say, Henry?"

He came back into the hallway with two mugs of coffee. "I said, Have a cup of coffee?"

"Yeah, thanks. A cup of coffee, thanks." I pointed to his new paintings. There was one of a guy in uniform floating in the sky. "Henry, you've outdone yourself with this one."

"Yeah. That's a good one. That's called *French Cop Caught in the Clouds.*"

"Ah," I said. "Where's Jane?"

"She's taking Rick to the vet." Rick was their wire-haired terrier.

"Is he okay?"

"He's got cataracts. Come on back."

I followed him to his office. I took the chair I took when I first came there because I was crazy. "Rick's pretty old, huh, Henry?" I said.

"He's older than me in canine age."

"How are you feeling, Henry? You okay?" He looked so tired.

"I've been a little under the weather. I'm old, don't you know?"

"You're in better shape than I am, Henry," I told him.

He shrugged his shoulders.

"So, Bayard, what's the beef? Girl trouble?"

"No, I don't think so. I thought everything was all right. But I guess it wasn't."

"What?"

"This girl I went with for a short while died."

I started from my relationship with Mary and went up through Ansil calling me. I even told him about the dream I had, and finally the letter. I handed it to Henry. He had an amazing feel for handwriting. He looked at a note my father had written me once and said, "Too many near misses in World War II."

Henry read Mary's letter and looked away, then read it again and handed it back to me. "She says it's nothing you've done. Did you do anything?"

"I honestly don't think I did anything wrong. I thought we ended it good. It was a healthy thing. That's what I took away from it. And I believed totally it was a healthy thing until this letter got to me."

Henry carefully took a sip of coffee. "Nobody killed themselves over you, Bayard. You're not that irresistible."

I made a laughing sound and went over to the window. You could see half of City Hall from it.

"Tell me about this Mary girl who thought she had to kill herself," he said.

I wasn't that much in touch with Henry during the Mary period. One reason was I felt healthy, so I didn't need him. Of course if didn't occur to me to call and see how he was doing. After all, he had only done more for me than almost any person I had ever known.

I told him everything I could remember about Mary.

"You never know what she had in her mind when she wrote this," he said. "She could have been drugged or have mistaken you for her parents or some guy she met on a streetcar in 1965. You could hold on to this letter and get sick or drop the charges against yourself, Sandy. Which, if you're asking my opinion, is what you should do. If you really don't think you did anything."

I nodded. "I swear to you I don't think I did anything."

"Your choices are to believe it or not."

"I don't even have any idea why she killed herself."

"Ego."

"Oh, I don't know."

"I'm sure it didn't feel like ego to her," he said. "I'm sure she had been trained by people with a vested interest to feel overwhelmed, which is what she felt. And it may even be that she might have been taking on the guilt of her runaway mother. But it was ego. Otherwise she would have felt sufficiently insignificant to go on living."

His left eye began to tear and his voice was weary from sitting there talking to me. He was phasing in and out on me, staring out the window.

"How are you feeling otherwise?" Henry asked. "Are you taking care of your money?"

"Yeah, Henry. I'm being pretty good."

"You working?"

"Yeah, and I'm taking care of my money."

"Actors," he said. He shook his head. "You all have too much time on your hands. Even the famous ones. They'll make a movie for three months then it's back to too much free time. You have to find a way to make a job for yourself, Bayard. Something you can do every day. Hamsters on the treadmill, they've got the right idea."

His voice trailed off in a couple of words I couldn't make out. For the first time since I had known him it looked as if his outside age was gaining ground inside. His mind was unable to stay put and help me. He asked me some weird questions about my parents and then interrupted my answer with a smile. There was pure love in his eyes.

"Did I say something crazy, Henry?"

"Bayard, you could still go either way, but I think you're gonna make it."

"You do? Make what?"

"If you can just keep your nose clean and play your cards right, this could be your last lifetime."

I stood outside Henry's building staring straight up for a long time. It had gotten a bit chilly and grey and clouds were moving together quickly like a mother-of-pearl puzzle. When I looked down again I saw a couple of Chinese kids wrapping a paper rope around each other. Suddenly I was starving. I thought of stopping into Hong Fat for some pork lo mein, but I didn't want to sit in one place too long. I didn't want to sit in one place and think. I didn't even want to sit in a cab. I ran through Chinatown and SoHo, home.

I tried to light a fire with a few sticks of wood I had lying around from the winter before, but I couldn't get one going. I must have burned an entire old Sunday *Times* under the wood. It just laid there and sneered at me. I lit the oven for some heat. "No heat, never any fucking *heat!*" The heat in my building only comes up for fifteen minutes a day anyway, and then only at two in the morning. I looked in the fridge. There was one English muffin, one third of a salami, one egg, and a milk carton half-filled with bacon fat. Why don't I ever keep any food in the house? Because you're worried you'll eat it and get fat, you stupid fuck! This is how I talk to myself.

I fried up the salami and toasted the muffin, made a sandwich out of it. It was actually good, especially with all the ketchup I poured over it. I washed it down with a glass of ice water.

Maybe I hurt Mary by not fighting to keep the affair together, even though we both were happy to end it. She even seemed relieved that I felt the same way she did. She wanted to go back to Ansil and I was feeling that it wasn't working right and I wanted to end it before it got bad. There was somewhat of a strain due to her inner, unresolved thing with him and . . . oh, what the hell was the difference? God!

I put a recording of a French singer I like, Barbara, on the stereo. The song I like the most on it has a line that means: but best of them all, my love, is you. Over my stereo I had a picture that Mary had drawn of me sitting in my bathtub wearing my reading glasses, holding a book. It's in black and white and done in one continuous line. Everybody who comes into my place mentions it. I looked at it until I couldn't look at it. Rain began to snap at the windows. I slapped my hands together. I looked through my pot box, but I was out of dope. Out of dope, out of mind, I always say, and leaned against the window ledge and played paddle tennis with myself, with one of those paddles with the ball attached by a long rubber string. I hit the ball eight times out of a hundred. It's my incredible eye-hand coordination.

I put the paddle down and sat on the couch. I was having an asthma attack. I was scared, I'll be honest with you. I hadn't felt so out of control since I was a kid. Up until I was ten or so I'd be off somewhere playing in the neighborhood and during a game of some kind I'd get so excited I'd lose my wind and black out. And that blackout panic was what I was feeling.

"No, no, you're not blacking out here. Okay, you could have done something to Mary but you don't think you did. Your chances of being accurate are as big as hers, and you're not even crazy." My wind started to come back. "Think things out, you won't die, you won't black out. Don't be such a pussy. Try to figure things out. You're entitled."

I decided I'd go see Mary.

There wasn't any hot water so I couldn't sit in the tub and think about why I was going. I felt better thinking I would go, so I was going. What was I gonna do, look at her grave? Even if I could find it? I'd have to call up the family to find out where she was. I didn't think it would be a good idea to give Ansil a ring and ask where Mary was located. I'd see her family and offer my condolences and as I was leaving their house I'd turn around and ask them, "Oh, by the way, Mary didn't happen to slip you a word on what it was I did to her that made her kill herself, did she? No? Oh, well, thanks anyway, have a nice day!" Maybe they would know, and finding out what I did had to be worse than worrying about what it was I might have done. Yeah, but I didn't do anything, all right? All right? Good.

I was going to call Ann and tell her I would be out of town for a day or two, but then I figured I'd call her from Boston. At least I'd be able to take a hot bath there. The temperature in my apartment had slipped down to a cozy twelve degrees. I called the Pinchot Hotel long distance and asked them if room 515 was available. I had been in a play in Boston and stayed at the Pinchot. Room 515 was available so I booked it for that night. I packed the black leather suitcase my father used to use to sell neckties through the South, walked over to my bank machine in Sheridan Square, and took out two hundred bucks. I had another two hundred or so in the house and took that with me too. I always keep a lot of cash around for escape purposes.

I got a cab going east and went out to La Guardia Airport. A guy from Trinidad was driving.

The time I lived in Boston was one of the best periods in my life. I had a large part in the play and after a while got to where I was pretty good. At every performance there were different usherettes from the many local colleges. They were theater majors. Their pay was seeing the play for nothing. I'd always get to the theater early just to see what was what. And I usually had good luck getting a date with one of them after the show.

I like acting on the stage. I look better from a distance anyway. I often took an usherette to Mr. Lee's Chinese Kitchen. Mr. Lee became a friend of mine. I gave him and his wife tickets to the show. Mr. Lee and I worked out a thing that when I brought a girl around I'd speak a little phoney Chinese to him. I sounded fairly authentic. And he would answer and talk back to me like he knew what the hell I was talking about. This would impress the girl no end.

"Sandy, where did you learn to speak Chinese?"

"Ahh, just picked it up."

We wouldn't do it if Mrs. Lee was within ear range. Mr. Lee felt she might not approve.

The airport was crowded with people returning

from the holidays. A lot of them had gifts under their arms. Priests were checking departure times. Married people were bending down over their kids, buttoning their new Christmas overcoats. Girls in L.L. Bean corduroys sat, hands folded, on chairs in the center of fortresses of suitcases and gifts, some waiting to fly back to boyfriends, some just waiting to be picked up by fathers.

And then there was yours truly. I was there too. I love Christmastime. And I was sorry it was over. I'm not gonna fully admit that Jesus died and then they put him in a cave and then he pushed the rock out of the way and then he left, or whatever the story is, but I do like Fifth Avenue just before it snows. And I like sitting at Rumpelmayer's drinking hot chocolate across from a girl with a cold winter face.

I went to a phone booth and called the stage manager at the theater and told him I was sick and to tell Victor not to get sick too because I wouldn't be there to cover for him. Not that that prick would get sick. But my job was safe for a day or two.

My plane was ten minutes away from boarding so I carried my bag into the drugstore shop, or whatever it's called, to get some nourishing food because it was close to six o'clock and I hadn't eaten since the salami. I bought a pack of Planter's Peanuts and one of those big round peppermints in the silver paper. I feel that your body is a temple. God loaned it to you and you should return it in good condition.

I always get to the boarding gate early to see if there's any pretty single women I can accidentally sit next to. But I didn't care this time. There weren't any, anyway—just businessmen reading the *Times*—the regular Boston shuttle–type group.

I did, however, sit next to a fifty-year-old businesswoman who was semiattractive, smoked continuously, and spoke in a mucus-riddled voice.

"I live in Dallas"—cough cough—"my boyfriend works in Boston. He's a hockey team executive." Hack hack.

She was kind of sexy though. She wore a skirt with a slit up the side which would even be a sexy look on Ernest Borgnine. Her breasts looked like they were still probably pretty good. Of course, airplanes make me horny anyway, no matter what. Museums too, which I've never been able to figure out. There's no fear of death in a museum. I felt my neck. My glands hurt a little, my ears were plugging up. "Aw, cut it out!" I said out loud.

I remembered an incident. It wasn't really anything that happened between the two of us, just something that happened to me.

I had picked Mary up at lunchtime to go skating at Rockefeller Plaza. That idiot Helen she was working for on Fifty-seventh Street tried to make her work through her lunch hour. She already had Mary staying late and coming in early every day. This is the same woman who referred to her own thirteen-year-old son as "sexy" and told Mary that she walked around naked in front of him.

Anyway, we went skating and Mary wore a little skating skirt, a little black one she'd brought along to change into. She could skate for real. I couldn't believe how good she was. It was something to see. I skidded my way over on my ass and asked her where she had come up with all that stuff, and she told me that as a kid she'd been good. So good, in fact, that there was talk of her trying out for the Olympics. After some huge woman skated into me backwards and almost broke my ankle, I yelled to Mary that I'd watch her from above. I handed in my skates and stood with a cup of hot chocolate on the terrace above the rink watching her. She had told me these things about being institutionalized and certain things about her father, the great healer, and her mother. I was thinking of those things while I watched her skate. I thought about her as a little girl doing figure eights on some frozen Massachusetts lake. I imagined what those big violet-turquoise eyes must have looked like then and how pretty her little-girl neck must have been. And I wondered how it could be possible someone could go off and leave a little someone who must have looked like what she must have looked like. It was then that the love I had begun to feel for her moved in a new direction. I felt responsible for her. It was a true love feeling. I suddenly felt the degree to which I could consider myself a good man depended on how kind I could be to her. She presented to my heart a clear case of right and wrong.

It was snowing when we landed at Logan Airport. I love Boston. It was so nice to me when I was there. It's a good luck town for me. I don't love it like I love New York, but I love it. I owe it a favor. I had carry-on luggage and so did the fifty-year-old woman. I sensed that she didn't want me to ask her for her phone number when she got in a cab and was out of there in three seconds. I found a cab and said, "The Pinchot Hotel. Do you know where it is?" A thick, Irish-looking young family man nodded that of course he did.

The Pinchot was a theatrical hotel and quoted cheaper prices to "artists." That's what it was back in the old days. But show business—the show business that's been so wonderful to me—has changed. Trained seal acts and husband and wife Apache dance teams once sat in the lobby of the Pinchot reading *Variety* and getting their shoes shined. But now it's pretty much limited to retired old men with purple noses.

I checked in at the desk. The clerk was a stocky blond guy in his early twenties with crazy eyes and ripe pimples marching out of the collar of his dirty shirt. I paid cash for the first night and took the key up to 515. It was a clean dump with very clean, very frayed towels in the bathroom. The ancient radio was still there too, just where it had been before—nailed to the table between the beds.

I looked for pubes in the tub, then ran a bath. I clicked on the old TV and waited for it to warm up. When the picture finally appeared it was a documentary on the proper way to fillet a fish.

I stood for a while at the steamy window by the bed and looked down at the street. I got very sad for a moment and thought I'd call my parents. But for me, checking into a hotel room and wanting to call my parents is like a knee-jerk reaction. I got into the tub instead.

I dried off about an hour later. It was about nine and I figured I could really do no Mary-oriented things that night, whatever it was I was gonna do in the first place. So I figured I'd go out and have a great dinner. I dressed well. You know, the grey-flannel suit, the one I got at Brooks Brothers. My pink cotton shirt and, of course, the tie that has sort of become a trademark for me. The dark black and blue polka dot. For shoes I opted for a simple cordovan loafer.

I was feeling a little lonesome and very hungry so I went to a place I'd been to once before called Durgin Park where it's noisy and everybody sits next to people they don't know. I ate prime rib, fried onions, and string beans across from a kidney surgeon and his wife. I phased out a time or two while the older couple told me about their trip to Europe. Maybe it was the wine, but I was thinking about dying. I can't imagine why. If I wasn't related to anybody and didn't have the one or two good friends I have, I wouldn't be afraid of death at all. It isn't that I'd miss them so much, it's just that they'd feel so awful about my death, for twenty minutes or so.

The doctor and his wife offered me a ride back to my hotel. It was around eleven o'clock. I had them leave me off at the entrance to the Public Garden near the Ritz-Carlton and thanked them. It was very cold and the wind numbed my mind. I went back to my room.

I took another bath and read the *People* and *Us* magazines I had bought at the Ritz. I watched Johnny Carson talk to Tony Randall, then fell dead asleep.

WEDNESDAY

I was up around nine coughing like Ratso Rizzo. My ears hurt, my throat hurt. I was sure I had a fever. But the day was bright and sunny through the window. I made myself shave and dress while I listened to a local Boston talk show on TV.

Host: Tell us who the mystery face is. We'll take the third caller.

I knew Mary's family's place was near the Henry Wadsworth Longfellow house. And I knew that that was close to Harvard. So I took the Red Line to Cambridge. It wasn't as cold out. The sun was all over the place. A lot of the college kids were still on vacation, although it was crowded around the square, with mothers shopping and teenagers sitting on the backs of bus-stop benches flipping lit cigarettes at each other and screaming in toothless Back Bay accents.

I had a cinnamon-and-walnut muffin at the Pewter Pot and some tea, and felt a little less incredibly sick. While the waitress went to get me more hot water I checked the phone book for the address. DR. WILLIAM RAWLINGS, MD. 1991 HAWTHORN STREET. His name made my stomach nervous. Because let's call a spade a spade here. I didn't know what the hell I was doing. What was I going to do, show him Mary's note? I took a deep breath, shook my head at myself, and paid up.

It was a historic yellow, three-story, wood-framed house. I rang the bell. It seemed quiet inside. The only car parked in the driveway was a '63 Dodge Dart. I recognize those cars easily because my brother almost drove over our high school football team in one during his driver's ed class.

That was the important thing running through my mind when a thirty-five-or-so-year-old cleaning woman and her blonde little girl opened the Rawlings' door.

"Yes?"

"Hi, my name is Sandy Bayard. I'm a friend of some of the family, uh . . . "

"Uh-huh?"

"And, uh, I'd like to find out if Jake Rawlings is around somewhere that I can get in touch with him. The doctor isn't around now, is he?"

"No. This is the doctor's day at the college hospital."

The little girl sucked her thumb and drooled on her mother's hem.

"Do you know if Jake is still in town or if he went back to school in Europe or if he's in the forest or something? He's a friend of mine. I haven't seen him since, you know . . . his sister's . . ."

This cleaning woman was not helping me out at all. Her little girl was trying to hang off her belt. The woman swatted at her head.

"There's a number on the board in the kitchen for the boy. Do you want me to get it?"

"Yes, thank you. Is he still in town then?"

She shrugged, as if having to clean that big crazy house up however often she had to clean it up was plenty without having to tell people who didn't work during the day about phone numbers for the crazy people who lived in the house. She was right, but what was I supposed to do—stop living?

She gave me a slip of paper with a phone number on it and no area code so I figured my good friend Jake, whom I'd met for twenty minutes in my life, was still in the general area. I thanked the woman and headed toward the hospital where her father's office was.

I was feeling sick, not from being sick, but from too many emotions. I don't think there are different kinds of emotions. There's just emotion or not emotion. I simply need calm, where you're at peace and can kind of understand the things you're thinking and be yourself. But my blood was boiling up like a wild Indian's. The way it had been when I was going downtown to meet Ansil. Too much emotion also makes me wheeze. And I'm not wheezing for anybody. Even if it means becoming an emotional zombie.

"Hello."

"Hi, is Jake there?"

"No, he's not. Who's calling please?"

"Who's this?"

"Liddie. Who's this?"

"I'm Sandy Bayard, uh—"

"Uh-huh."

"I was a friend of Jake's sister, Mary. And I'm just . . . well . . . all I'm really . . ."

"Oh. You're Sandy, the actor from New York?"

"That's right. Yes."

"Jake's mentioned you."

"Oh, uh-huh. Well . . . all I was . . ."

"I'm Liddie. I'm Jake's girlfriend."

"Oh? Uh-huh."

"Jake went off camping for a while."

"Oh, he did?"

"Yes, I don't know how long he'll be gone. What are you doing in town, Sandy? I remember Mary mentioning you."

"Really?"

"Oh, yes."

"To tell you the truth, uh . . ."

"Liddie."

"I'm in just to get out of New York for a day or two, Liddie. Just really to go somewhere else for a day or two. Also, just to call or to maybe see Jake and give him my, you know, condolences. Maybe we could have had a drink together, me and Jake. I don't know. It was a spur of the moment kind of thing, you know. You know me. I was once in a play here in Boston. It was a couple of—"

"Do you have plans tonight, Sandy?"

"Uh . . . what?"

"Do you know people here? Are you staying with friends?"

"No, I'm staying in a hotel. I just came in for a day or a few days or so, really. I don't—"

"Well, I'm working in a department store."

"Uh-huh."

"But I haven't got any plans for tonight, so are

you doing anything tonight, Sandy? If you're all alone here . . ."

"I'm totally free. That sounds great, you know."

"Great. I'm home for lunch now. I really gotta hang up and get outta here, but . . . do you know where Harvard Square is?"

We made a date to meet at a restaurant there at eight o'clock. Okay, for some reason I was relieved. Sue me.

I hung up the pay phone and strolled around Harvard eating a box of lozenges. I felt like I had just found an extra twenty dollars folded in my wallet. To be honest I was relieved that Jake wasn't in town. Because if I were him I maybe would have begun not to want to talk about it. Mary's father, I forgot about him. The lozenges made me nauseated. To settle my stomach, I sat on a planter between parking meters.

Just before I got the job in the show in New York I was very broke. And for some reason nothing gets me crazier than being broke. I didn't come from a poor background. Just the opposite. And not only that—my dad has always helped me out if I need money. He'd mail it up to me with a note clipped to the check saying: HERE KID, THIS SHOULD HELP TAKE THE PRESSURE OFF. LOVE, DAD.

But when you're close to thirty you want to take money from home as little as possible, unless you're Vincent van Gogh or somebody. And I'm not even Vincent Sardi. I was still with Mary when these money worries were upon me. I owed money from when I was out of work so I said to her once, kind of half kidding, that it was driving me nuts. And she said, without looking up from a book she was reading, "When they stop letting you on the bus, that's when you know you're going crazy."

I laughed when she said it because it's a great line. But she didn't say it like that. She said it like she had done some thinking about it and she was giving me the benefit of her knowledge from a secret map. I remember sitting down across the room from her and thinking, okay, she's cracked. I once asked the psychic about Mary, whom he had never met, about why people had been cruel to her at such a young age, and why so many bad incidents in a row were heaped on someone too young to bring them consciously or unconsciously upon themselves. And the psychic said that maybe in another life Mary had been a Gestapo agent in a prison camp and had tortured people and she was getting paid back in this life. Now I certainly don't believe that, but here's what I think: either the psychic is right or there is no reason for it. I honestly don't know which is harder to accept. Because then it's every random man for himself. Because then it's possible to smoke cigarettes and not necessarily get cancer and die. It's not one hundred percent, it's not written. And just because I'm in show business and work it out so I stay in it fifty years doesn't mean I'm gonna naturally get famous after a point. Or that people I know who have had it seemingly easy and who make a lot of money and who are irresponsible and get too stoned to show up for work on time, that history won't necessarily teach them something.

When the nausea lifted, all I had was a tubercular cough and somebody's death on my conscience.

"You came here to do something, so go do it!" I said out loud in a tone that, if someone else used on me, I'd never talk to them again. I stood and walked toward Mary's father's hospital. It felt better to be walking. I put Mary's letter in my hand but I didn't look at it. *It's nothing you've done, but it feels like it is.*

I always tried to make sure Mary had cab fare or

I'd go get her if she was working late. She'd go around New York with twelve cents in her pocket. It would drive me crazy. All we ever did was eat Chinese food and watch "The Honeymooners." She had never seen it before. She went wild over them, especially Alice. She said she'd never seen love depicted as completely as Alice's for Ralph. And as schmaltzladen as it was, Mary called me Norton and I called her Ralph. We were always doing bits about Alice being in the other room while I planned to sweet-talk her into giving me her household money for some scheme like overnight pizza mailing companies or whatever. Mary would get so happy and giddy. As if there was a slumber party of nine year olds going on inside of her.

"Dr. Rawlings is having lunch," said a pretty Oriental receptionist-nurse.

"At a restaurant?"

"Up in his office, second floor, across from X-ray. He brings his lunch in a paper bag." Her nose crinkled in reverence for the kind of bag he brought his lunch in.

"Thank you," I said. I went to the elevator. Nobody stopped me. My heart was pounding. I pressed ten. I was too nervous to press his floor right away.

Something happened at the halfway point in my relationship with Mary. That point of no return in a love affair. The place where you realize you might as well keep flying in the same direction because it would take the same amount of fuel to turn back. Mary had cooked a pasta dinner for me and two married friends of hers. She had the dinner at my place because it was a little larger than hers. They were grad students or young teachers or whatever at Harvard. The husband was gay and the wife didn't mind. This isn't conjecture on my part. Mary told me so. "They have an odd relationship," she said. At least the husband was a woman, I thought. At least he did something. The wife looked completely sexless. Not unpretty. They were both pretty. She was just sexless looking, in the way certain feminists are sexless because they don't want to be manipulated.

The evening was not a million laughs. Mary was very nervous about whether or not they would like the food. All they would give her was an occasional "Interesting . . . interesting taste." I was being nice. I didn't care about those two. They were infinitely better educated than I but that doesn't scare me. I'll get around to all that. No. Besides, I get a kick out of hearing about books and facts I don't know anything about. But all night long all this couple did was play the parts of the people they were supposed to be. Real boring. They really made Mary sweat, these two "friends" of hers. They obviously didn't approve of her work. And they certainly didn't approve of me. Maybe I'm exaggerating. I probably am. But not much.

Mary had something in her that made her believe people like them saw her correctly. After Mary had cooked this delicious meal and heated their goddamn bread for them, after which they said it wasn't "warm," but they'd eat it anyway, and after they drank this expensive after-dinner brandy I bought that came in a cedar box, and after they looked around my apartment like it belonged to a child because I didn't own any plants, they put on their coats to leave.

Mary and I did the dishes and I tried to make her laugh. But she was too sad and began to cry. To see it made me feel the way you feel when a child accidentally hits its head against something. You want to go up to whatever it is the child hurt itself on and kick it and hit it with your fists. "The meal was terrible," she kept saying.

"Hey, honey." I took her hands out of the dishwater and held them. "Are you crazy?" I said. "That was the best goddamn meal I ever ate and I've eaten better fucking food than those two friends of yours ever have."

I wanted to shock her and get her to stop sobbing because it was sad.

"Christ's sake, honey, those two people aren't good enough for you. They don't deserve to be eating your grub. I should tackle them on Eleventh Street, reach my hand down their throats, and yank your food back up."

I did get her laughing after a while. But still . . .

This sort of thing happened to her a few more times from more of the same kind of friends. They didn't always make her cry, and some of them were nicer than others, but none were gems. The easiest thing to say is that she probably felt she deserved these people, but who knows? It hurts to say it, but I grew angry with her after a while and it wasn't just because I hated to see her get hurt. No. I got mad when she would prefer to be with those people. It made me feel unappreciated. I felt I was losing her attention by being nice to her. She trusted me and knew I was safe, that *I* wouldn't hurt her, but other, meaner people, *they* had to be conquered.

The elevator stopped at the second floor. I tried to be angry enough at Mary not to be scared of her father but I wasn't. Dr. Rawlings's name was on the door across from X-ray. My cough was bad. I could hardly swallow. All I have to do is offer my condolences in an absolute and sensitive way, I thought. Any more than that, I just play it by ear. Okay. I was ready to knock.

A firm "Yes?" was heard from behind the door.

I pushed the handle down and went in. Dry, crisp Mozart was playing at a civilized volume. The lights were dimmed.

"Dr. Rawlings?" He was bald and lying on a green leather couch with his eyes closed and his hands crossed serenely on his chest.

"What please?" eyes still closed.

"I'm sorry, sir, you're resting. I should have called . . ."

He opened his eyes. "What is it?"

"I'm a friend of Jake's. I've come to offer my condolences."

I couldn't say Mary's name to him right after waking him up. He might kill me or something.

"I'm . . . I was a friend of your daughter's really, sir, and I just wanted to pay my respects."

"What's your name?"

"Sandy Bayard."

He rose a bit. He was small but square like a longshoreman. He wore a white short-sleeve shirt and a seersucker tie. And I remember thinking that it was winter and he was wearing a seersucker tie.

"Are you related to Coddy Bayard? He lives in South America now."

"No, Doctor. Uh-uh."

He was disappointed.

"I interned with him in New York. He's a brilliant man." He said that to me as if I had been related to Coddy. "I asked her if you were related to him, did she ask you too?"

He remembered Mary went with me. Could I ask him about the note, just play it by ear?

"No, Doctor, no. She never did ask me if I was related to him."

He was smiling at the thought of his friend. Then he looked uncomfortably at the steam coming out of the big old radiator. "Jesus Christ, they keep it hot in here." He crossed the small office to the window and lifted the shade. The sun pointed into the room. I could see his still-full lunch bag on his desk. He raised the wide window and turned back to me. I thought he was going to ask me what I wanted again.

"I won't keep you, sir, I just wanted to offer my sympathies, sir . . ." My voice was fluid and sick sounding. I had a white, cold sweat on my forehead.

He nodded at me. "You got a cold?"

"No, I'm fine, sir. Really. I just wanted . . ."

"You got a fever?"

"I think so."

He went to the foot of the couch he was sleeping on, opened his medical bag, and brought out a thermometer. He walked over to me shaking it.

"That's nice of you, Doctor." I really did feel bad.

He put the thermometer in my mouth and sat me on a hard chair. He sat on the corner of his desk and picked up a heavy red medical book.

"She cried and cried when you weren't dating. She liked you a good deal, don't you know?"

He was trying to give me a compliment. He said it nicely.

I almost swallowed the thermometer. She was CRYING AND CRYING. Am I nuts? I don't remember anything! I mean, it was painful and it was bittersweet to stop seeing each other, but there was a feeling about it, as if we were doing the most evolved, loving kind of thing . . . but maybe she wanted me to stop us from ending it and I didn't. And she cried and cried. I moved the thermometer to the side of my mouth.

"I hope I never hurt her, Doctor."

I was very scared. He didn't seem to think I did anything wrong. He just gestured to keep the thermometer in.

"Did you see her mother? Did you see her brother?" He hadn't said Mary's name yet.

I shook my head. He looked down at the big red

book. Then he pushed it away from him and took the thermometer out of my mouth. He looked at me before he looked at it.

"He's very rude to my present wife." Out of nowhere, there was this angry spit in the corners of his mouth. He went to the window light and twisted his body around the thermometer.

"Oh, I'm sorry," I said, referring to Jake.

"You're a couple of points up. Sore throat?"

I nodded. "And my ears are plugged."

He took a prescription pad and a little pen out of his pants pockets and scribbled on it.

"I'm sure, Doctor, that you're all in a state of shock. Jake probably doesn't know—"

"For years"—he interrupted me—"for years the same shit." Resentment was boiling in the words as he handed me the prescription.

"Thank you."

"You should rest."

His phone rang. "Yes, please? Ina! How are you, sweet girl?" He was pleased. I don't think he had any sense that I was still in the room. "Of course we do. Call my wife and fix up a time for you and Burton to come by. Please do, sweet girl . . ."

I swallowed a lot of coughs in a row trying not to interrupt his call. I felt so bad. I wanted to get out of there. He finished on the phone.

"How long the cough?"

I told him just today, the cough. I wanted to get the hell out. Being sick left me with no resistance about Mary. And this thick, tough old man had me totally off balance. I had no sense of how to be with him. I couldn't remember ever feeling that way about anybody. I coughed again and couldn't stop.

The room was still hot. He took my elbow and guided me to the open window. He turned me toward the light, put his head half an inch from mine, and peered into my eyes.

"She was the same way." The crazy spit back on his mouth. "When I think of how respectfully she behaved with her mother, and her mother walked out, don't you know?" He looked at me and waited.

"Uh-huh."

"My sin was not becoming romantic to them by leaving. I stayed and raised them."

I was taller than he, and he pulled my head down slowly and took my neck in his hands.

"Your glands are swollen." Leaning down over him like that, my ears stopped up, making me dizzy. He continued to feel around my neck and just above my collarbone, hard. He was hurting me.

"I wasn't romantic to you. I should've left too. Then I wouldn't have the shit-assed looks at my wife."

I swear on my life he said "you." I was dizzy and less than half a foot from the open window. It was just the second floor, but it was a tall building. I almost fainted. He walked back toward the center of the window. He was writing out another prescription.

"Take this too." From the look on his face it didn't faze him that he said the things he said.

My hands shook in the elevator, and for the whole time I waited for my prescription to be filled.

Later I floated in the hot hotel tub for over an hour, a little high off the cough medicine.

As I was getting out of the cab in front of the restaurant, I saw a girl looking out from behind the glass doors. It was Liddie. She had long, light brown curly hair and a girlie cellolike figure. She wore a leotard and her full breasts were right under it. She had a flowered skirt tied around her waist that was silky and clung to her when she moved forward to meet me.

"Hi, are you Sandy?" she asked.

"Yes."

I had slept most of the afternoon and hardly felt sick at all. Actually, I felt as if I looked like Oskar Werner. We went over to the bar and sat at the end. The restaurant was more crowded than the bar. Liddie sat to my left, which is, after all, my better side.

The first part of my life was spent in my room listening to Frank Sinatra records. The more recent part of my life is spent in my apartment listening to Frank Sinatra records and in bars stretching the truth with someone new. I wasn't on a date, but nine out of ten times you are on some kind of date.

Liddie offered me a low-tar cigarette, which I took, then she lit us both up.

"I thought you were gonna be older," she said.

"I intend to be. I didn't know what you looked like. I forgot to ask. Would you care for a drink?"

"A glass of wine?"

I hesitated because of the antibiotics, but I ordered one too. Liddie had pink London girl cheeks and her mouth had a permanent smile.

"Liddie, it's nice you could have dinner with me. I really didn't know anyone here anymore."

She clinked my wineglass with hers.

"You mean you didn't come to see anyone or anything in particular?"

I shook my head. I thought of saying, I thought I'd go out and see where Mary's buried. Maybe that's why I came to Boston. I honestly don't know what I'm doing, but I do it well though, don't you think?

She smiled and gulped down the rest of her wine. I was pretty sure she had dressed up for me. I had the feeling that she liked me about a half an hour before we met. It was then that I got the Henry Diaz emotion. I first got this feeling when Henry Diaz, this poor Cuban kid from another neighborhood, came to my brother's twelfth birthday party. Everybody else gave my brother gifts like model planes, milk-white Rawlings baseballs, or a collection of Chip Hilton sports stories. But Henry Diaz gave my brother his entire comic book collection. It was quite a collection too. There was the first issue of *Superman's Pal Jimmy Olsen* among them. Many of the comics were yellowing but all were in perfect condition. Henry was so happy to be invited to this party that he wanted to give my brother something extra special. But his gift was passed over. Or else it made the kids embarrassed because it wasn't a "bought" gift. It was a poor boy's gift.

I had gotten the Henry Diaz emotion and suddenly I wished that Liddie, Jake's girlfriend, whoever she was, had not dressed up for me.

"It was such an amazing thing to happen. Everyone was so stunned. There's no way to describe it," she said.

"Mary?"

"Yes. Jake found her. The next morning. He had to run up to the bedroom where he and I had spent the night and pull me down to the pool house to see her because he couldn't talk and someone had to call the ambulance."

"Because of his stutter."

"Yeah."

"Did something particular go on that weekend?" I asked her. "Was there a particular incident that might have finally pushed her into it?"

"If anything she seemed happier or, actually, more like hyper happy than I'd ever seen her."

"What do you mean, 'like'?"

"Well, she was telling us all how good a time she was having and she was nostalgic about the house. She talked to me for a long time about the wonderful memories she had of growing up in the house. But after a while she seemed like she couldn't stop talking about it. She went on and on, faster and faster, like a top.

Since our table was ready, we moved from the bar. I ordered a bottle of wine and we changed the subject. Liddie wanted to be in the theater. We talked about laughing on stage when you're not supposed to. We talked about a play she had done in Boston and how "it really was a very professional production."

By the end of dinner we had finished the bottle of wine. After a couple of drinks at the bar we were both drunk. She asked me to walk her back to her apartment which "wasn't far." The waitress took the money for the bill and I excused myself and headed for the men's room. On the way there and out of sight was a pay phone. I called Ann collect. She was probably still at the theater. When I got back Liddie was talking to one of the waiters, who had gone to college with her.

"Sandy, this is Lonnie Price. We did *The Rainmaker* together at Tufts."

We finally left but not until after I'd heard about how Lonnie had given up the theater.

"I'm going to finish grad school and if I still want to be an actor later, there'll be plenty of time. And besides . . ."

Everybody is an actor now. The insanity is, it's often those guys with Lonnie's kind of arrogance who do better than a lot of people with ability. It never occurs to them that they might be rejected. And if they are rejected, it never occurs to them that the guy rejecting them might be right. Just turn on your TV and look at all the actors making a million bucks who are bad at their job. Then, the great part is (after *People* magazine puts them on the cover), they begin talking on any subject because people listen to well-known people. Maybe I'm jealous, but I'm not interested in having the time-space continuum explained to me by the cast of "Growing Pains."

By the time we got to Liddie's apartment I was dead again. She had macramé on the walls. She also had one of those nervous little dogs that some girls have.

"Just let me feed Robespierre and I'll be right back. Make yourself comfortable," she said.

Robespierre's odor was giving me asthma. I looked around. There was not one thing in the little apartment that had anything to do with Jake. He probably just slept there once in a while. Who knew?

"We're back," Liddie yelled, stepping over the dog food as the mad, crazed, six-ounce Robespierre charged up on the couch where I was sitting and got his hair all over my pants. Okay, I'm going nuts, I thought.

"Would you like a cup of tea, Sandy?"

"Uh"—a hard sneeze—"yeah, a cup of tea, good." Then I yelled at the dog in a whisper, "Try taking no for an answer." He started gnawing and scraping at the cuff of my only decent pair of grey pants. "Liddie, can we put Robespierre somewhere . . . like in the refrigerator or something?"

"Robespierre!" she yelled at him. But the dog didn't care. Liddie came over and picked him up and took him into the kitchenette with her. The little crumb looked back over her shoulder at me and smirked.

"I'll put you in the fuckin' radar range, you asshole," I sneered at him under my breath.

I was wheezing. "Actually, Liddie, could you give me a cup of instant coffee instead?" The caffeine speed sometimes makes my breathing easier. Maybe it was the too-small room that was giving me the asthma attack. Maybe it was the last two days. Maybe it was what I was going to ask Liddie, but probably it was just the fucking dog. The result, no matter what the reason, was that old nostalgic lung pain I first encountered at age six when the lungs felt like they were stuffed full of flaming, humid cotton balls.

Liddie brought in the coffee after penning Robespierre in the kitchenette. He kept yapping every other second. She flicked the overhead light off and lit a big, lumpy, many-colored candle that was placed in the middle of the driftwood coffee table. I gulped the coffee down and instantly burned a hole in the top of my mouth.

Liddie had slipped the hem of her silk skirt above her knee. Robespierre must have sensed this because he gave out an ugly, high-pitched whine from the other room.

Liddie went over to her records and bent over to select one. She was so feminine. No wonder artists wanted to paint women.

Did Mary's father try to dangle me out the window? I was going nuts. My lungs were going fast. When I was a kid and I'd black out with asthma I'd wake up in our bathtub at home, my dad wiping my hair back off my forehead with a cold sponge. And sometimes I'd wake up in the car on the way to the Variety children's hospital. When you're a little kid and you feel an asthma attack sneaking up on you, you get nervous. And the more nervous you get, the worse you wheeze. It's a permanent effect knowing that at any moment your body could betray you. You can't turn your back on yourself for a minute.

Liddie had put on some strange jazz. I wanted to find a drugstore and get one of those nonprescription asthma inhalers.

"Liddie, where is Mary buried?"

"She's not, Sandy, she's—"

"*What?*" For one stupid, chilling moment, I thought she might still be lying in state.

"She's not buried! She was cremated."

"Oh, cremated."

What an awful thing to have done to you. I know it's absurd, but I thought, what if Mary needs her body when she gets up to heaven, what's she going to do—have somebody carry her jar around?

Liddie told me Mary was in the Royce Mausoleum. I can't tell you why, but somehow I didn't feel as compelled to visit her vase.

Liddie sat down too close to me, which I sort of hated her for.

"Liddie, could you do me a favor?"

"I'll try."

I got up and paced the room. "Could you think back and see if you can recall Mary ever mentioning me in any way? I know it may sound strange but, you know, when somebody you cared about dies you want to make sure you did right by them . . . you know, anything she might have said about me?"

Liddie looked up at me like nothing was weird about my asking her that. Which also made me sort of hate her.

"Well, Sandy, she told me you were an actor—this is when you and Mary were seeing each other or had just started seeing each other—although you didn't see each other that long, did you?"

"No, uh-uh!"

"I have an interest in the theater so I remember that. I saw Mary at Thanksgiving, and I remember I asked her about you, if you were doing any plays in New York or how your career was going, because I've given some thought to going to New York to study, although I'm not sure when I'd—"

"Yeah, but did she say anything about me then when you asked her that?"

"She was back with Ansil again then was she not?"

Was she not? *Was she not!* What the hell kind of way was that to talk? I was dying for clues and I was getting was she nots!

"Yes, she was back with Ansil by then—yes!"

"Well," she continued, "I remember this one thing—"

"Yes? You remember this one thing. Yes?"

I was scared now because something in me said Liddie might just say *anything*. I was a little cracked right then and was now wheezing my ass off. Liddie was talking to me as if she were auditioning.

"Well, Sandy, you had been broken up however long you had been broken up, and I asked her how you were doing and she wouldn't answer me. I asked her a couple of times."

"She wouldn't answer you? What do you mean?" I sat down next to her.

"She just cleared some plates off the table and didn't answer me. She tried to make it look like she wasn't hearing me, but I knew she could hear me, she just didn't want to answer my question. Why I remember it was she *wouldn't* talk about you. I'm sort of sorry to tell you this Sandy, but she started talking about Ansil."

I nodded, feeling as if I were going to cry. She went on.

"Mary told me all about a big heart-shaped box Ansil had given her. He had filled it with all different little gifts. Bath oil pearls, a little mirror, a Winnie the Pooh notebook, candy . . ."

My heart was pounding.

". . . I remember it so much because of how clever it was. Mary really wanted me to appreciate Ansil for it. I remember that."

"Liddie, I gotta go, I've got to find a drugstore and

buy an inhaler. I'm not feeling too good. I'm wheezing a little bit. I think I may be allergic to Robespierre. It's mutual anyway," I said. "I just gotta go, Liddie. I'm sorry. I've had a real nice time."

I couldn't stay there any longer. Liddie apologized about mentioning Ansil, but it wasn't that. The thing was, *I* had given Mary the heart-shaped box with all the romantic things in it. This should've made me feel better. Mary was really crazy. Why would she say Ansil gave it to her? Did she really think he did? She was back with Ansil and wanted Liddie to like him. That could be it. But why wouldn't she talk about me? All she had to say was we really cared about each other but it didn't work out. I didn't know. Who knew?

Out on the street my breath came back. I took the Red Line back to the Pinchot. When my lungs stopped burning I went down to the sleazy bar off the lobby for a drink. I needed one to calm down. Of course I fully expected the alcohol to interfere with my breathing the instant I swallowed it, but hey! There were five loiterers in the place—one was the huge black bartender who poured me the world's smallest glass of tequila, one was a ninety-year-old gay man who was playing the score of *Hello Dolly* on a pea green upright piano, and the rest were customers. I think one of the customers was dead so I shouldn't have counted him as fully there. He sat straight up in his chair with his head thrown completely back. He was like that the whole time I was in the bar.

I drank my first tequila in about a quarter of a second and asked the bartender for another. He had an expression on his face like he might give me another one and then again he just might not.

I gulped down my second tequila and looked around. The piano player was going for the award. He was really trying to entertain. I began to feel a little warmer and airier inside. There was a phone booth on the other side of the room. I motioned to the bartender that I'd be right back. He was thrilled to hear it. I called Ann.

"How ya doing, Ann?"

"Sandy, where are you?"

"I'm in Boston. Thought I'd pop up here for a day or two. I don't know if you noticed it or not but I've been going a little screwy . . ."

"Sandy, guess what? You're not going to believe this."

"What?" I thought she was going to tell me that Victor Sprigger had gotten sick or drowned.

"They closed the play!" she said.

"Yeah, I know. I told you they were closing it in a week or so—"

"No, they closed it tonight. Everybody's going to get their two weeks final pay. The producer had another run-in with Mitch"—Mitch is the great director—"and she said 'Close it tonight,' so nobody even has to come to work tomorrow."

"Jesus Christ!" I said. "She's crazy, that woman!"

"Yes, she's refunding tickets. She doesn't care. I think she's going to start a lawsuit against Mitch."

Mitch must have called her a cunt again. He must have called her a crazy Spanish furniture-heiress cunt—that would drive anyone over the edge.

"Ann, this is a great fucking business we're in, huh? I don't care though, how about you?"

I was glad, I didn't want to go back there, ever. I couldn't stand standing-by anymore. I couldn't have taken another week of it, especially after what was going on with me. I was feeling like I couldn't stand anything.

The elderly piano player was standing by the phone

booth, waiting to make a call. "Listen, Ann . . . how are you doing? I've been going through some weird—"

"Sandy, I'm leaving town tomorrow."

"You are? Where are you going?"

"I told you I was thinking of visiting my parents, didn't I?"

"Oh, yeah." I hadn't remembered.

"They're wintering on Maui. They're there for two months and they invited me so I'm going to fly out tomorrow."

"Tomorrow? Don't you have to get a passport?"

"Sandy, Maui's in America."

"Oh. Yeah. That's great Ann. How long are you going for?"

"A month maybe."

"Oh, yeah? That long?" I said. "We'll miss you, you know."

"Will *you*, Sandy?"

"Sure!"

"Yes, sure you will." She said it in a way that for her was pretty nasty.

"Look, Ann, have a good time. Mambo sounds—"

"Maui!"

"Yeah, Maui, it sounds great. Have a real good time, you know?"

She was trying to zing me for reasons I most likely deserve because I'm such a lousy bum. But I was cracking that night and I didn't give a shit.

"Okay, Sandy, I'll write you from there. I'll miss you and take good care of yourself."

"You know me, Ann!"

"Yes, I know you."

She didn't have to say that. "Say listen, Ann, write me with your phone number and I'll give you a call. Okay? Take care of yourself, kid."

"Oh, and Sandy?"

"Uh-huh?"

"Your friend Ansil called looking for you. I told him I didn't know where you were."

He probably wanted to drop over and punch me for slamming him before he walked out of Ann's.

Ann said good-bye again and we hung up. I stared at the phone and the numbers scrawled on the wall in a semidaze.

"They're organizing, Sandy, old pal—all the women you've ever known are organizing to pay you back!" I said out loud. I looked up and saw the gay pianist still looking through the glass partition of the phone booth. He was watching me talk to myself. I stood up and walked out of the booth saying, "It's a good phone. Worth waiting for," as I passed.

I was on my way to total drunkhood. I had had the wine with Liddie, and now the tequila was taking hold. The bartender had another one set up for me when I got back. But I remembered the antibiotics and didn't drink it. The dead man still had his head thrown back and another couple had come in. They were in their fifties and looked as if they had met in a diner. They smiled at me as I sat down again. There was nothing swingerlike in it, just friendly. Although I'm sure I was completely wrong about their motive for smiling.

Ann was sad about leaving me, but I think it was probably the best thing. The relationship wasn't working out, to coin a phrase. Ann had been as nice to me as always and I liked her and respected her as always. But I had been wanting to get out. There was nothing I could point my finger at. Not a lot that could help me not feel like a prick. But I didn't love Ann. Maybe I had become more aware of that fact. It was good that she was going away. She wanted out of it too. I don't know how I came up with it, but my theory was this:

it was hostile of Ann to take such good care of me because I truly didn't feel I was even half the love of her life she acted as though I was. Actually she didn't act like that. She acted as if she didn't want me to see what she really thought—that I was the love of her life. I felt like the guy in *The Iceman Cometh,* the drunk, who finally kills his wife because she kept forgiving him for coming home drunk.

This was how I had perceived my relationship with Ann before Mary's death and subsequent letter. And as I sat there, in the most depressing bar in the galaxy, trying to perceive things that way again, I only succeeded in convincing myself that I hadn't been right about anything for twenty years.

Anyway, no matter what, Ann was off for a month. Tomorrow's headline would read, HE'S AVAILABLE LADIES. The Mayor would award me the key to the perfume department at Bloomingdale's.

My breathing got heavy again. Not with wheezing—it felt as if the air around me was thickening. It was taking all of my strength just to breath it in. I drank the tequila. Fuck it.

"Maybe Ann's the one," I mumbled to myself. "Maybe she's the one and you've totally fucked up the rest of your life. Maybe Mary was the one and you fucked up her life and your life and Ann's life."

The piano player started up again. This time I thought he was playing one of his own compositions. I left the bartender a huge I'm-sorry-about-the-slavery-thing tip and walked out of the bar into the lobby. The same pimply guy was behind the desk.

"You're from New York, right?" he asked me.

"Yes, uh-huh."

And then he smiled at me strangely. "You ever go to the motorcycle bars back there?"

All right, this is great, I thought. He's a rough trade homo with a passkey to my room. Just what I need to worry about—getting boned by the night clerk.

He was still smiling at me like a werewolf.

"No, I don't know anything about those kinds of bars."

I got into the elevator and pushed five. Once in my room I pushed the heavy oak dresser in front of the door to protect myself. I was as close to going to an asylum as I had been for some time. And might have gone, except I'd have to pass the guy in the lobby.

I floated on the outskirts of sleep.

THURSDAY

The second I opened my eyes I decided to go home.

What was left of my cold lifted as soon as I saw Eleventh Street. It was still morning so I bought a copy of *Rolling Stone* and went over to the Pink Teacup for breakfast. They have the thick bacon there that I'm so famous for liking. I came back to my apartment about an hour later and, bless my soul if I didn't get a call from my agent. Actually, it was my agent's second-in-command. A young guy named Michael, who wasn't from Great Britain like my agent but saw no reason why that should stop him from talking with a British accent anyway.

"Ummm, Sandy, they're casting a television pilot at NBC today. You're right for one of the nonrecurring roles. Can you go and have a meet today?"

"Sure, Michael."

"Sandy, you're reading for the role of Steven. It only shoots one day."

He gave me the name of the casting guy and what floor it was on and the time. I asked Michael what the pilot was about.

"It's a sitcom about a family in New York in the 1930s during the Depression."

"Sounds pretty funny."

It actually didn't sound too terrible. It was a semi-provocative idea at least. I mean, it wasn't as wonderful as, say, a show about nasty "yuppie" doctors in a supposedly poor hospital who think they're hipper than their patients and the viewing audience. But comparison, you know? Comparison'll kill you.

I was supposed to be at NBC at three. I was happy to have something to do, something that could make me some money too. Michael had said they might pay a few bucks over scale should I "win the role." Should I win the role! I don't know why the hell I'm an actor, I hate the goddamn business so much. I hate so many of the people and yet there's never been anything else I've ever wanted to do. No, I'm lying, I don't always hate it, and as bad as most of the people are, they're better than most "outside" people. The money, when you make it, is good, the acting beats working for a living! But for the last few years I've begun to feel embarrassed about doing it. I'm not always a great actor but even when I don't stink I'm still always more talented kidding around backstage. Even if I were to get famous, which of course is all anyone wants out of life,

I would still be working for other people, standing where other people tell me to stand, saying what other people wrote. That would be okay, though, because I'd be making a million bucks and have socialites chasing me all over the place, so I could live with that, but what if I don't get famous? What am I going to do? Play the dating interest on "The Golden Girls" when I'm sixty-two? I'd really get a great feeling of work well done then! But when I think about the people going to office buildings on hot subways at eight every morning, their armpits chapped from the heat, I see I don't have a whole lot to complain about.

I called the stage manager of the show and got the official word it had been closed. I tacked up a note on my bulletin board to go to unemployment.

Around two-fifteen I took the subway uptown. A couple sat across from me, looking at a map. They were both blond and very beautiful. I figured them to be in their early twenties. When the boy took off his gloves to turn the page of the map I saw a gold wedding band on his finger. Why is it that only the plainest, simplest things mystify me? Looking at those two lucky surpluses of nature set me off thinking about guess-who for the sixth millionth time.

People, mostly those who have never felt too bad, always say they don't believe you when you tell them you'd change places with people who seem to have better luck than you. They always say, "Oh, but it's all that trouble that makes you who you are. You wouldn't want to change that." *Of course* I'd like to change that, or give it up to be a very handsome, rich person who never got sick. Life is only how much pleasure you get. Everybody ends up in a box under a stone that other people turn away from as they drive to the airport. There are people for whom it's all easy and who are easy in themselves. There are people who think mostly about what to do and where to go. And then there are people who think mostly about what they have to do in order to get out from under the weight of themselves before they do anything. Their thoughts are tangible, weighty things. Thoughts killed Mary. Things that aren't even present killed her. It did her no good being smart. If anything, it made her even more aware of her inability to shut her mind down.

I walked from the subway stop on Forty-ninth Street, east to Rockefeller Center. It was cold and grey outside. I'd planned to get a slice of pizza before the audition, but decided to wait until after because I always get food on my clothes and I didn't want the producers thinking I was the kind of guy who, once they hired him, might get food on his clothes.

People were skating in Rockefeller Center. Girls with sexy legs and behinds, the old guys in love with themselves because they could skate backwards. I didn't look very long.

Even though I was a little early I went up to the appointment. I didn't know any of the five other actors in the waiting room. Usually you know somebody. But I didn't know anybody. I was the only blond guy there. There were a couple of women too. I didn't know them either. One girl was borrowing the other girl's hairbrush. And a couple of the guys were pacing up and down opposite each other in the hallway, mouthing the lines of the script to themselves.

I looked around for a secretary or someone to say I was there. One of the actresses said, "They come out and get you."

"You're telling me," I said.

"What?"

"Oh, nothing. I was just . . . are there any scripts around?"

"Yeah. She'll come out and give you one."

"Thank you."

The actress looked eighteen, but you can never tell. She had a summertime dress on even though it was nine degrees outside. I don't think I'm telling tales out of school if I said I felt like doing adult things with her breasts. I was going to talk some more to her, but she went back reading her script. There was no extra place to sit so I took my overcoat off and laid it on the floor. I brushed my hair with my fingers looking in a mirror above the secretary's desk as I sat on my coat.

A fat woman in thin women's jeans came into the waiting room and called in one of the actors. I said, "Hi, I'm Sandy Bayard," to her from the floor and she handed me a script.

"Sandy, you'll be reading the role of Steven, the encyclopedia salesman, on page fourteen through the middle of page sixteen. Let me know when you're ready."

I browsed through the script and read over the pages a few times. Steven's lines were filled with things like "Mrs. McSorley, someday I'm going to get out of encyclopedias and make a million bucks." The show was called "The McSorleys" and what it was was a way of showing how happy a family should be without money.

I put the idiotic script down and looked at my hands. Mary always liked my hands. She told me I had fingers like Jimmy Stewart. *Mr. Smith Goes to Washington* was her favorite picture. I felt so low I almost walked out of NBC. Here I was sitting on the floor waiting to act and all I felt inside were real things. I got nauseated and a little dizzy. I swung my head around violently and took in a couple of deep breaths. The other actors looked at me. They thought I was getting in character.

Something happy kept me from fainting. I remembered the time Mary stood up to me and told me off. Well, Mary's version of telling someone off. I had stayed the night at her house and she'd gone off to work, made me coffee and eggs while she was dressing, while I was still on my ass in bed watching "Today" on her little black and white. Anyway, after Mary left and I'd waved to her down on the street, I turned on her record player without turning off the TV, which always blew out the power in the apartment. She had warned me often enough about this but I'd forgotten. The fuse boxes were down in the basement and I didn't know how to find them or fix them, so I left her a note saying I was sorry, figuring she'd do it when she got home. Mary and I had made a date to go to a seafood place on Jane Street for dinner. She got home at six and around six forty-five I was rereading one of my favorite Kennedy assassination books in the tub, happier than a clam, just grooving, thinking I'm the best boyfriend any once-institutionalized girl could ever have when Mary called me.

"Sandy, I certainly believe you might have . . . at the very least . . . maybe you could have at least replaced the fuse. I think I'm right about this. Or you could've met me here and held the flashlight in the basement!"

She was right, of course. Things had gotten so good with us and Mary seemed so happy that my natural, lazy, "spoiledness" surfaced. I went right over. By then she had the lights back on.

"Boy, you're right, Mary. You stood up for yourself. I admire that about you . . ."

She was grateful that I hadn't turned it back around to make it seem that somehow she'd done something wrong. She reveled in a normal beef with a normal person. It was a little incident, but her posture even seemed better that night.

A couple of weeks afterwards we decided to end it. Or she decided. She had begun to see Ansil again. She said that he had come up to where she was working. She seemed bothered by his unannounced appearances, which made me feel free to say, "Tell the bum to cut it out!" But she'd sort of apologize for him and say, "He just thinks it's so unfinished between us." It made me angry and jealous—and the depth of those feelings alone were almost enough to make me want "out of the relationship." But there was one more layer to it. Mary looked so sad in her role of The Loved One that it startled me into behaving correctly.

"Ansil came by the office again, Sandy."

"He did?"

I had just picked her up from work and we were walking back to her apartment. She had been kept late as usual and looked terribly tired.

"Yes, he came up around lunchtime so we went out for a glass of wine."

"What's going to happen, Mary? Are you going back with him? You can level with me."

"Sandy, let's have a drink at my place."

I knew it was coming, and I'll tell you the truth, I was relieved. Being with Mary even for the short time I'd been with her took a great deal of energy and concern. Being with myself has always taken even more energy and concern, so I really couldn't see how she and I could go on together. But there was love there and so a great part of me wanted us both to act otherwise.

At her place she poured us two large glasses of Remy Martin.

"Would you hate me terribly much if we just became friends for a while, Sandy?"

I was sitting far back on her bed with my legs dangling over the edge like a kid.

"This is what you want to do, huh, Mary?"

"Only if you'll continue to be my dear friend. I need you to be my dear friend."

It was such a corny phrase to use "Dear Friend," now that I think about it. There've been other women who had told me the same thing just to make it easier for them to give me the brush, but Mary said it as if it were taking out a big loan on my love for her.

"Of course I'll always be your friend, Mary. I love you."

We had two or three more Remys and got pretty emotional with each other. Yet never straying too far from the truth. I told her it was the best affair I'd ever had and how I had only good wishes for her and she told me how good I'd been to her. I know she told me that, I know she did. We parted that night without sleeping together. I remember standing at the street corner in front of her second-floor kitchen window—her waving down at me and blowing me a kiss. I didn't call her for weeks afterwards. I wanted her to get back into her life with Ansil and frankly didn't care to feel the pain of hearing her voice, no matter how movie beautiful it ended. She called me, though, a few weeks before I spotted her and Ansil in that rainstorm on Fifth Avenue. She said she just wanted to see how I was, and we small-talked for a while. The funny thing is I remember feeling some anger toward her because she sounded so happy and on top of things. I guess I felt she should be suffering a little more without me. Christ!

"Huh? Oh, yeah. I'm ready. Sure."

It was the fat girl asking me if I was ready to audition. The other actors looked around as if to say, why the hell was I going in before them? The fat girl led me down the hall. There were rows of secretaries. Each looked up from their typing as I passed, saw whether or not I was worth anything, and then went back to their typing. Above all their heads were large color photographs of NBC television stars.

We finally got to the audition room and the girl knocked on the door. A thin, bald man with a very trim beard opened it. He had on a plaid workshirt and jeans and work boots. He had a red bandanna tucked neatly in his back pocket. This man was in charge of casting.

"Hello, Sandy," he said. "I'm Todd Masters and this is"—he pointed to a fat man in a suit and an attractive brunette woman sitting on a couch and introduced me. She was pretty. They were both producers. "I'll be reading with you, Sandy," Todd Masters said.

"Is there anything you'd like to ask about the script?" the man on the couch asked me.

"No, I guess it's all sort of self-explanatory," I said. I wasn't trying to be flip or funny, but they laughed. I still wasn't nervous. I was so stretched out of shape emotionally by that time that I was perfectly relaxed and pretty funny. When I started acting I just did whatever came into my mind and after a minute or so I saw I was going over. It's funny how loose you can be sometimes. The pretty woman on the couch was really reacting to me. In part of the scene I was supposed to flirt with the McSorley daughter, so I started flirting with her. I wasn't sucking up to her for the job or anything. I was just loose and funny and basically didn't give a shit. If more of my ex-girlfriends had killed themselves I'd probably have an Academy Award by now.

By the time I got through reading my lines I was sitting on the couch with my arm around the woman. I was good. I've stunk before on many occasions so I know when I'm good, and I was. They told me they'd most likely be calling my agent today as the scene I was up for was shooting tomorrow. I was given a script to take home, which was a good sign. I thanked them and left the office very casually and politely, but also like I couldn't care less if they called me or not, because God forbid you should want the job. Even if you're the best choice for the part anywhere on earth, if they see you want the job they'll give it to someone else. It's like a poor guy wanting a free meal. They'll kick the guy in the ass and run him out of town. But should that same guy inherit a million bucks no one will let him pick up a check.

When I came out of the audition room the other actors and actresses gave me the fish eye. I felt like saying, "Pardon me for living, everybody. My guts have been turned inside out for the last week and today I got a couple of laughs. And you're begrudging it to me." But I didn't say that. I wished all my colleagues good luck instead, because that's the kinda guy I am. I'm that kinda guy.

I took the elevator down, bundled up, and left the building. No announcements came over the loudspeaker saying, "Mr. Bayard is leaving the building." But that didn't stop me, I left the building anyway. I felt good. Maybe I'd get the part and make some money. I'd never gotten a job so soon after another job ended. I was always down to the last two hundred bucks of my savings before I ever hooked another job. Sometimes I wouldn't even hook one then. But hey, I'd do it all for nothing because I happen to love the business.

It had warmed up even more and I decided to do some walking. I went over to a Bun 'n' Burger and had two of their great hamburgers with all the melted cheese on top and a Coke.

Around five I was back at my place, trying to take a nap. My cold was gone, but my back hurt from the lousy hotel mattress. I have a bad back anyway from a motorcycle accident I had in high school. I was doing Marlon Brando impressions on a friend's BMW and fell and skidded all over the teacher's parking lot. Considering how far I skidded, I was remarkably unhurt. My back still tightens up on me every other day or so, though.

Anyway, I was lying on my bed trying to close off my mind and sleep when my agent called telling me I had the gig. I was going to shoot the next day and earn two grand. My agent now liked me all of a sudden and Britishly congratulated me. It was my real agent too, not the flunky Michael, who usually talked to me. I was glad I was shooting the next day. The more I rehearse, the worse I get. I put a Segovia record on the stereo and started a bath. There was hot water in the building again. My luck was turning.

I looked over my lines in the tub and wondered for a second if I should plan out a way to play the part. But I hadn't planned on anything when I read for it, so fuck 'em. I washed my hair instead.

I felt much better than I'd felt in what seemed like years. I knew it was because I'd gotten a job and was going to make a chunk of dough, but the fact was, that right then I wasn't scared of Mary, which was reason alone to celebrate.

I didn't want to sit alone all evening watching public television so I thought I'd call somebody. Maybe there was a party going on someplace. Who did I know I could call? I didn't know anybody. Calling Ann seemed out of the question. I knew a couple of guys I could call to find out what they're doing, maybe hang out with them. But who was I—Marty? I gave my friend Bolley Clifford a ring.

"Clifford, how ya doin'?"

"I'm doin' good. Who's this?"

"Bayard. Who's this?"

"I didn't recognize your voice, Sandy," Clifford said.

"Well, it's me, trust me. What're you doin' tonight, man? Do you have a program for this evening? What's goin' on?"

"Well," he said, "Marsha and I and Marsha's sister and her fiancé have tickets for the famed acrobats of Taiwan."

"Marsha?" I asked him.

"Marsha. My girlfriend."

"Oh, I didn't know you were going with someone, Clifford. Since when?"

"About three months. You met Marsha at the party we had."

"What party? I came to a party?"

"Yes, you came. You got real drunk."

"Jesus. Did I meet Marsha?"

"Yes, you met her. Don't you remember, you got drunk and told her that she looked like Steve Cauthen, the jockey. Do you remember that?"

I started laughing. "I don't remember. Did I make her mad? I'm sorry, I didn't mean to. Cauthen's a very nice-looking jockey."

"Yeah, well, it bothered her. Then you got sick in my bathroom."

"For Christ's sake, Clifford. I'm sorry. So come down here and puke in my bathroom. But don't kill me here. You know, come down here, both you and Marsha, and walk in my closet and puke on my clothes."

He laughed. "You're a piece of work, Sandy. You know that? You're a fuckin' piece of work."

"Yeah. So I'm sorry your girlfriend's mad at me. Tell her I'll make it up to her. Tell her I'll put a lot of money down on her at the Preakness."

Bolley laughed again. "So how you doin', Sandy?"

"Oh, man, I've been goin' through some stuff. I've been goin' through some very original things. But tonight I thought I'd have some fun, y'know?"

"Yeah. You okay? What's goin' on?"

"Aw, it's too crazy. I'm fine. I just wanted to do something tonight. Distract myself. So you're booked up, huh, Clifford? You're a booked up woman, huh? What'd you say you were doin'?"

"The famed acrobats of Taiwan."

"What are you, crazy now, or what?"

"No, Marsha's sister and fiancé invited us. Take care of yourself, Sandy, I gotta go. Check the sports on Channel seven. It's women's ice skating. Look at some skating ass. That should cheer you up."

"Okay, Clifford. I'll talk to you soon, okay?"

"Yeah. Talk to you soon."

I hung up and put the TV on without the volume. I still had the Segovia playing. Tai Babalonia was skating with her partner. How beautiful women are. The lines of their bodies are a force of nature as powerful as food. It was too much to look at. I turned off the set.

I daydreamed a little about the McSorley's pilot getting sold and me being asked to be a regular—the show becomes a big hit across the country and Sandy Bayard dolls are made and teenage girls hide under my bed in hotel rooms. But then I stopped thinking about it. The networks make hundreds of pilots a year and only about six of them ever get on the air, and half of one ever gets to be a hit.

I thought of calling my parents and telling them, but my dad always gives me about two hours of "Do the producers like you, kid? Are you sure you got the job? Did you sign the contract? Do your agents like you? Do you have a lot of lines in the thing, kid? Does the director like you, kid?" And then my mother always gives me two hours of "Didn't I tell you when you were a little boy you'd be famous? Didn't I?" So I decided I'd tell my parents about it in a couple of years.

I decided I'd go up to the Palm restaurant and have the world's greatest steak. I really felt good. I'd get a great steak, some of their incredible fried onions, maybe a whole bottle of wine, by myself.

I got to the Palm around eight and had to wait forty minutes for a table, but it was worth it. Afterwards I bought a cigar and walked uptown. I was going to go to this comedy club where my friend is a regular performer. But then I remembered that I had to get up early. I turned around and walked back downtown. I really felt like getting laid. I wanted to share my good news with someone.

I was pretty drunk. I had had a whole bottle of wine. "I'll share this day with myself. How about that?"

I went home and played some records, took a bath, and went to sleep. I dreamt that I said to somebody—I don't know who—"You can't measure the weight of someone's soul on the bathroom scale." I don't know what it meant, but I dreamt it.

FRIDAY

I had my coffee around seven. Jane Pauley was on with a consumer activist. He wore a cheap suit and had one of those bad haircuts to prove he wasn't a crook. I glanced over my lines while I watched.

I was at NBC twenty minutes early. An assistant director met me and took me to makeup. The makeup guy already had someone in the chair—a beautiful blonde actress with a man's name—what else? I went to get a cup of coffee in the studio we were going to tape in and there I met another actor in the show. His name was Barry Seif and he was bigger and heavier and darker than me. He played one of the McSorley boys. We shook hands. I was even more relaxed after I saw how nervous he was. I could tell he wanted to be a sensation. Let's keep our fingers crossed for him.

"It looks like we have a pretty good script here, Sandy," Barry said. He practically stood on top of me while I poured myself some coffee.

"Yeah, I guess so."

"Did your agent settle on good money for you, Sandy?"

"Yeah, I think they settled on halfway decent money. Of course," I said, "I won't be keeping any of it."

"Huh?"

"No, I'll turn all my fees over to the Will Rogers Institute or the Retired Actors Home. That's the way I am."

"Oh, come on," Barry said.

"I'm just kidding."

"So, Sandy, your agent made a deal for you?"

"Yeah." I couldn't wait to get away from this guy. He looked like somebody from Seattle or somewhere. One of those guys who get into acting because they see it as a good business venture. A way for them to buy land or own their own boat. Those guys usually do end up actually owning land or their own boats. Me, I'll actually end up at the retired actors home.

I watched them darken Barry's fat neck and kidded around in front of the actress I was going to act with. She was standing in front of the mirror moving individual strands of hair on her head around like she was operating on a child's heart. I started doing this bit I do sometimes when I have a lot of cash on me. I still had a lot of my Boston money. I pulled all the twenties out of my pocket and stuck them into Barry's shirt while he was being made up.

"Barry," I said and squeezed his face, "Barry, all I'm asking you to do is just don't be as good as I know you can be. Walk through your role, pal. Let me steal this son of a bitch and you'll be lighting your cigars through silk, bambino." I squeezed two twenties into his hand. The makeup guy thought it was funny. Barry gave me a phoney laugh and said if I didn't watch out he was going to keep my money. The actress told me I was crazy. Crazy.

Mary made me a party on my birthday. My friend Tony from the show was there and a few other people I really like. She laid a great table—the tablecloth, the napkins, the food all arranged in colors van Gogh might have chosen if he had ever been happy. She put orange light bulbs in some of the lamps making all of us in the little room feel like we were all on a summer country lawn watching our children swim. Bottles of champagne. She had twelve different kinds of bagels and a homemade seafood cream cheese. And around the big, beautiful country bowl of cream cheese she placed little, clear plastic rainbow-colored fish. Whales, lobsters. It was those plastic fish. They are what showed me how big I loved her.

They were going to tape my scene first, and suddenly I was afraid I might cry during the comedy.
The actress's boyfriend came into the makeup room while I was being made up. He was a skier type, very handsome. He took hold of her shoulders and talked to them.
"Relax. You gotta let your muscles go."
That was his job—to talk to her shoulders.
I wanted to get my scene over with before I became the actor who once he's hired gets sad enough to

be committed. They in fact didn't shoot my scene until five in the afternoon. By then I pretty much felt human again. The assistant director came to get me, just as the makeup guy got through with my face for the second time. The director came out of the soundstage to meet me and the actress. You've seen this actress in a lot of soap commercials. She's always getting advice on the best way to get stains out.

The director had us rehearse the scene a couple of times. I was so tired from waiting and dodging thoughts about Mary that I just did what I felt comfortable doing. Apparently that was all right because halfway through the second rehearsal the director said, "Let's make one." We did one take through and it wasn't too bad. The actress and I were all right together. There was even a place in the scene where it was supposed to be a little tender moment between the two of us and that went all right too. Right after the tender moment I got a laugh from somebody behind the camera because on the spur of the moment I sat on the actress's lap. Anyway, I wasn't asked to do it again, and the producers came out with the director to thank me, which was nice.

When I got back to the makeup room, Barry Seif leaped out of nowhere and asked me how it had gone. Barry had been through shooting hours ago but had hung around. I told him it went all right. I wished him luck, he wished me luck. I wished the young actress luck, she wished me luck. I wished her skier boyfriend good luck, he wished the actress's shoulders luck, and I was out of there.

I was on the street by six and really bouncing back, I have to admit. I had a good feeling about my performance. I walked over to a Sony place on Fifth Avenue and looked at the color television sets. I was on one of them, thanks to a video camera they had for sale. I still had my makeup on.

I got in a cab and went home. I was so tired from the whole day I fell asleep twice in the tub. I'd had a few doughnuts at NBC but no lunch because I was profoundly full of despair. I finally pulled myself out of the tub and fell into the bedroom. I was asleep by the time I made it to the bed.

I had a dream in which I was planting rubber explosives under the big hotels in Miami Beach and I eluded the police by escaping through a tunnel of nicely tailored overcoats.

It was eight o'clock when I opened my eyes and looked at the clock. The apartment was dark. I clicked on the reading lamp. The buzzer rang. Somebody was downstairs. The sound of the buzzer gave me a jolt and I was up and out of the bed answering it before it stopped. I switched on a couple of lights before whoever it was came up the stairs.

"Show business!" my friend Jack Park shouted up to me from the floor below.

"J.P.!" Good old Jack. The guy always shows up at the right time, I swear to God. Nobody better could have rung my bell just then. And he just shows up too. He's never had his own apartment. He stays with people. You can never get in touch with him. He's an artist, a cartoonist, and very good too. But he always has to take some job to make money, which he never has any of. It's always a job that when you call to get him, they don't know where to find him.

Jack and I met at an actor's benefit of *A Chorus Line*. God, what a bad show. An entire play about how interesting and complex dancers in musical comedies are. I couldn't believe my eyes. I went with an actress I really wanted to sleep with who wanted "more than anything else" to see it *again*. We sat in the last row of the balcony and it still wasn't far enough back. My date ran into a girlfriend of hers who was seeing Jack. We all went out to eat afterwards. Jack took me into the men's room with him to smoke opium. We ate everything in the restaurant and laughed. Jack's sense of humor is to say everything as if he's a guest on the "Tonight" show.

"Yes, Sandy, things are *marvelous* and the kids down at the office, well, we're more like a family down there."

Or I'll ask him when he's by himself where he'll be living next and he'll say, "Well, Sandy, *we'll* probably be staying up at so-and-so's house, and he's a genius."

"Jack Park, this is great. What are you doing here?"

There was a girl following him.

"I don't think the folks at home know that I'm just down the hall taping my own special and I heard you kids were in here doing your own show . . ."

When he got up the stairs he kissed me and turned around to the girl and said, "I gotta explain this. In show business all the men are homosexuals and we kiss."

The girl Jack was with was loving it. "Sandy Bayard, we, and by we I just mean me, want to introduce a little lass, a gal by the name of Canada. Canada, a hell of a good Joe, Sandy Bayard."

She was very, very cute. About nineteen or so. She looked like Leslie Caron. She had her hair in a punk cut and wore one of those fur jackets that remind me of the flying monkeys in *The Wizard of Oz*. We shook hands. "It's nice to know you."

"It's nice to know you."

I helped Canada off with her coat. Her figure almost stopped my heart. She was small and graceful and lush. Jack took off his too-big navy blue overcoat and spun around like he had just finished singing "Feelings." Jack is dark and small, thin, and balding a little on top, but handsome in a beat-up way. There is also a deep unhappiness in him.

He wore a button on his shirt that said VISIT BEAUTIFUL JACK PARK.

"Geez, it's good to see you. I'm glad you came by," I said. "I don't have any beer or anything. I'll go out and get some."

"No, don't," he said. "We're going to get some dinner and hear this new band tonight. And you have to come with us because the weatherman's predicting unusual fun."

"Oh, yeah? Who you gonna hear?"

Canada answered. "Jimmy Van Dan and his Perfect Strangers down at this new wave place, the River Club."

"Oh, yeah?" I said. "I've always wanted to see that club. Gee, that'd be great. I've been going nuts around here. I'd love to do that. Things have been . . . yeah, that'd be great. I'd love to do that."

Jack smiled at me and leaned down to look at my records. "Yeah, these guys are good. I'm gonna be doin' the artwork for their first record. Jesus, Sandy, you have the worst records I've ever seen. Why don't you get some Jerry Vale records and, you know, really complete your collection? Yeah, you'll like these guys, Sandy. They do a song called 'Let's Go Out to the Lobby.' "

"They do a really great song about the movies, called 'Bruce Dern So Long It Looks Like Up to Me,' " Canada said.

I said, "They sound great."

"Good musicians, too. Crazy charts. Those kids write crazy charts."

Jack picked out a Van Morrison record and put it on. Canada was looking at the things on my mantel.

"You have a lot of great stuff here."

"Thanks."

"Canada lives near you. That's why we came to get you," Jack said.

"Oh, yeah? Where?"

"On Greenwich Street, right above the Big Wok Chinese restaurant."

"It's a three-flight wok-up," Jack said. "No, no, I kid the Chinese people. I kid the Chinese people and an hour later I kid them again. But as you know, Sand, I do it out of a love and out of a respect and out of a thing . . ."

Canada smiled a very nice smile at him.

"Well," I said. "Are you guys hungry? Are you ready to eat right now? Do you want to go?"

"I'm hungry," Jack said.

Canada nodded her head in agreement.

"Okay. Let me just change my shirt. Make yourselves comfortable, look through my desk, do anything you want. I'll just change my shirt and punk the look up a little bit."

I went into the bedroom and unwrapped a new white shirt. I felt a little nervous. As if I hadn't been around people in weeks. But I was so glad Jack had come over. It was as though he was there to give me a transfusion.

"What do you do, Canada? Are you working or are you an artist as well?" I shouted out at her.

"Uh, right now I'm looking for a job, really. I was working as a secretary for Columbia Records. They only hired me temporarily so now I'm looking again. I'd like to find something in music."

Jack said, "Sandy's an actor. I've never seen him act, though. But he's a genius at the craft of acting."

I tucked my shirt in and came out. "I'm a ready human person."

We headed over to a place on Seventh Avenue I go to every now and then called Monterrey Pop. The food isn't good, but it's an alive room on a weekend. There was no wind but it was cold on the street so we didn't do a lot of talking. Canada was up ahead of us a few feet, bobbing up and down as she walked. Friday night in the Village, even on a cold night, is always a mob scene. I don't like to go out that much on the weekend. I like to leave the weekends for the civilians. Being the usually unemployed crumb that I am I can go out any night of the week. People with regular jobs are too rough on Friday and Saturday nights. They're trying too hard to squeeze a week's worth of something into Friday and Saturday nights, and they scare me.

But on this night I wanted the hysteria. I needed to be out. The bar area of Monterrey Pop was as crowded as the restaurant area. But there was one booth near the jukebox we grabbed. The speaker just above our heads was playing Elvis Presley's "Don't."

"Is this okay for everybody?" I asked.

"Just fine," Canada said.

She was taking off her coat. Jack and I both helped her out of it. She was still as beautiful under the coat at the restaurant as she was at my apartment. I hadn't noticed her eyes before. They were pale brown.

We sat down. "Jack, is this a satisfactory dining area for you?"

"The consummate booth, the booth's booth. I think we should be drinking."

"We should definitely be drinking. We should be drinking," I agreed.

"Ummm," Canada agreed too.

The waitress came over, a very tall, tough waitress who it seems is always my waitress no matter where I sit in any restaurant or what time I come in.

"Hi, how ya doin'?" I said to her. "How ya doin' tonight?"

"Fine," she said. A real no-nonsense waitress.

"Good. We'd like to order some drinks and then we're gonna do some eating. Okay? Huh? Uh, I guess we could order food now too, you know."

"Let me get your drinks first and come back for your food order after I get the drinks."

Jack did a take like she had suddenly scared him. Canada laughed and put her head down to hide it. Jack ordered a Johnnie Walker straight up and draught beer. We decided to all drink the same. Canada asked where the bathrooms were. I told her and she excused herself.

"She's great," I told Jack when she left.

"Isn't she cute?"

"Where'd you meet her?"

"At Columbia Records. I had to go up there to show the art director my portfolio for this Jimmy Van Dan record and she was a secretary up there. We've been to hear some bands a couple of times."

"So you're doing that dating kind of a thing, huh?" I asked him.

"No, no. We're just friends. She's just a friend of mine. I'm still dating Marisol. She's down in Sarasota for a week with her kids."

"Oh. So you're still seeing Marisol. That's great. That's been going on a long while hasn't it? Kind of an ongoing thing, right?"

"Over a year now," Jack said. "That even amazes me. I don't think I've ever been with anyone for as long as a year."

"Marisol must be great. I don't really know her that well, but the few times I've met her she's been very nice to me."

"Yeah. We get along."

"That's good," I told him. "I can't see you staying somewhere where your old lady's chucking rolling pins at your head."

"No, no."

I wanted to ask more about Canada but I didn't know what to ask and by the time I thought of something she was already weaving through the tables on her way back. We all bullshitted for a while and when the drinks came we lifted our shots of whiskey and looked at each other.

"I'd like to propose a toast," I said. "To you two folks. I appreciate your inviting me along tonight."

Jack put his hand on my shoulder and said, "It's wonderful to have an entertainer of your caliber along with us."

Canada touched our glasses and drank to our health. The shots were hot and we chased them with the beer.

The table closest to us had eight fairly heavyset young women sitting around it. They were doing a lot of laughing and seemed to be really enjoying themselves. I could gather from bits of their conversation that they all worked in the same office or office building. One of the women was sort of the ring leader, or head comedienne. She looked like she must have organized the evening. I could hear her say things like, "No, no, I told him I wasn't going to take any of that. I told him so. I said, 'Mr. Borghauser, I'm not a criminal. I can't work Saturday. We have that racquetball game against Pedestal Fabrics and I'm not missing it.' " Another one of the girls got hysterical and asked her, "What did he say then? What did he say to that?"

The waitress returned to take our dinner orders but we hadn't yet looked at the menus she'd left. Canada handed them out. Jack told the waitress we wouldn't let her down again and then ordered another round of Johnnie Walkers. We all decided to get the stir-fried Szechuan steak and salad. When the waitress came back she put down the drinks, took the order, and was gone before I could ask her for a glass of water. We clinked glasses again and knocked back another one. The whiskey felt good in the wintertime and the beer was quenching and cool.

"Are you from New York, Canada? No, of course, you're from Canada probably, right? I should be a detective the way it only took me two hours to put that together."

"I *am* from New York," she said. "My parents were from Canada. From Montreal. But I grew up in New York on the Upper West Side. Where are you from?" she asked me.

"I'm from Florida. From Coral Gables. Right near Miami, you know?"

"Uh-huh."

"You're not going to believe this, but they call me Canada too," I said.

"Isn't that amazing?" said Jack.

Canada laughed and shook her head at the amazingness of the coincidence.

"I'm kidding around," I said. "They barely even call me by my real name down there."

"Where?" Jack wanted to know.

"Coral Gables, Florida," Canada said.

"Oh, that's right," he said. "Sandy's from Florida. I've never known anyone from Florida."

Canada asked me when I'd moved up north.

"Practically the day high school ended."

"I love New York," she said.

"Me too."

Jack started singing "I Love New York" and snapping his fingers like Frank Sinatra. I was feeling good from the drinks. The three of us stopped talking for a while and looked around the restaurant. The customers seemed to be in harmony. Even the colors of their winter clothing seemed to match from one table to another. I watched Canada look around. I thought about how exciting it would be to get into bed with her, about how long I'd like the love to take. But I also thought about how fine it felt just the way the evening was. I wasn't going to make myself all nervous trying to work toward a reaction from her and ruin a good night with two good people.

The food came after a long wait and was the usual bad food it always was. But by that time we were halfway into the bag anyway, so it didn't matter. It was still too early to go down to the River Club so we had another round of drinks at the Monterrey Pop bar. We took our beers and whiskeys over to the jukebox. Jack excused himself to go to the men's room by saying, "Sandy, you know how I hate leaving before the end of a show. But I'm doing a benefit for Danny's St. Jude Hospital." Then he kissed us and went to the john.

We turned around after he walked off and stared at the list of songs on the jukebox.

"I like Steeley Dan," she said.

"You do? I do too."

I put my hand about a foot away from my head. "Lyrics out to here." I put money in and pushed "Deacon Blues."

Her little hands were spread out over the lit-up glass of the machine.

"Hey, they got 'Teddy Bear' here," I said. "Do you like Elvis? We can play some early Elvis."

"I don't know his early songs that well. I don't really know his late songs that well either."

"Yeah, well," I said pressing the Elvis button, "The first time Elvis was on TV in *King Creole* I remember my brother and I staring at this guy, looking back and forth at each other and getting excited like, finally here's something for us, you know?"

"He's when rock and roll started."

"Yeah. Up until then it was Patti Page and Frankie Laine. Doris Day singing 'Once I Had a Secret Love.' How long could that kind of stuff go on? 'Cause it could stunt your growth."

Somebody had brought their little girl into the bar. The cutest little blonde girl all wrapped up for winter. She was taking peanuts out of the bowls on the bar, climbing down carefully off the stool, and handing the peanuts, one at a time, to the customers. She handed me and Canada one nut each. We thanked her and made a big fuss. I told her I was going to save my peanut and have it for breakfast tomorrow morning. She liked that and brought me another one about five minutes later, for lunch.

The three of us kept drinking with one another until it got late enough to go to the club. We got a taxi and piled in. Canada was in the middle. Jack pulled a huge joint out of his pocket and lit it up.

"I didn't know you were holding, man," I told him.

"Man, I'm always holding. Even when I don't have any dope I'm holding. Can you dig the consternation?"

"Yes."

"Well, then," he said holding out his hand, palm up, to me. "Miss me entirely."

I very smoothly slid my hand by his without actually touching it. Then he handed me the joint. He offered Canada his hand and she missed it entirely. He was going to offer his hand to the tough-looking Puerto Rican woman who was driving the cab but thought better of it.

"My only worry," Jack said, "is that we might be too hip for the room by the time we get down there. We might put everybody up tight. So let's de-hip a little before we arrive."

"We're too hip already to start de-hipping now," Canada said.

We pulled up to the club just as we were finishing

the very strong grass. I don't know who paid the driver, or if we paid her at all. I'm sure we gave her at least twenty bucks too much.

There were a group of punkesque kids hanging around outside the place, sneering and looking bored and staggering around with cans of beer. I liked the way they looked. There was a lot of humor in the best ones; in their clothes, the way they were thought out, symmetrical. Some of the boys came out of their punkness long enough to look at Canada.

There was a long bar just inside the front door. I paid a huge, terrifying-looking man five bucks each for Jack and Canada while they were looking around.

"You didn't have to do that," she said.

"I know that, but you guys can get it next time."

"Okay. Thanks."

"It's a pleasure. It's just great to be here."

"Sandy?"

"Yeah, Jack."

"Did you pay for me too?"

"Of course."

"You're a god."

We found an area for ourselves near the end of the bar and ordered three beers. Jack ordered a shot of whiskey with his and Canada said, "You sure drink a lot."

And he said, "There's a lot to drink."

Canada insisted on paying for the drinks. The River Club was one huge room with giant columns lining the walls and an extremely high ceiling. There were no tables and chairs. The bandstand seemed to be about ten or fifteen years away. There were a lot of people there—about half of them punkly dressed, I guess you would say. There were also SoHo-ites, rich-looking, slim, thirty year olds with small belts and Marlboros. The rest of the crowd was just people.

Jack told me that the first band we were going to

hear was Metric, which featured a girl singer. He hadn't heard them before. Jimmy Van Dan would follow.

Somebody was adjusting the Metric's equipment before their entrance. We three leaned our backs up against the bar and looked around. Canada put her arms through both of ours. The stage lights came up and the voice over the loudspeaker said, "Welcome Metric."

The group was made up of four guys and this averagely sexy little dark-haired girl in a black leather jumpsuit. As soon as she came on stage, before the band played, Jack said, "I think this is the best group I ever heard."

It turned out to be not too good. She sang strongly, but there was nothing really interesting in her voice. And she kept taking sexy poses, just in case you missed the fact that she had on black leather. But it was exciting to hear a live band.

Jack went over to talk to one of the members of Jimmy Van Dan's band. I finished the last of my beer and turned back toward Canada. She was looking at me. There were new pretty things in her face every time I looked at her. I put the empty bottle of beer down and tried to order another one, but the bartender was way down at the other end of the bar. Canada put her bottle of beer in my hand and watched me while I took a drink from it. When I was through she turned back to face the bandstand. And in the same motion, put her right arm around my left.

Metric got a mild response. The bass player gave the finger to somebody as he was leaving the stage, and then the lights came up. Jack came back with a crowd toward the bar. He didn't look as drunk and wasn't reeling as much as when he left. I think he'd had a snort of coke. He kept inhaling loudly though his nose. He stood in front of me and Canada and told us exactly what he had told us before, that that wasn't

Jimmy Van Dan and his Perfect Strangers we just saw. That Jimmy Van Dan and his Perfect Strangers were next.

The bartender finally came down to our end. We ordered three more beers and Jack saw someone else he knew and took off before the drinks came.

"Beautiful Jack Park," I said.

Canada smiled in his direction and said, "He's an original."

"He's one of the sweetest guys in the world," I said.

"He doesn't seem very happy," she added.

"Maybe. But he has some fun. I thought maybe you and Jack were . . . you know. I didn't want to intrude on anything if you two were—"

"We're not. Not at all," she said. "I really like Jack. He's great. But he's going with someone. And I just stopped seeing someone. And we're friends, Jack and I. I think we'd just be friends even if he wasn't seeing someone."

"Uh-huh," I said. "He's a good friend to have. He's like an outlaw who always sneaks back into the town he's wanted in just to make sure his friends are okay. If that makes any sense, which I don't think it does . . ."

"No, I know what you're saying," she said and looked at me.

I looked back at her, right into her eyes.

After a second or two I put my hand up to her face. She leaned her head up and we kissed. She looked up at me again and turned around. The other band was coming on. I put my arm gently around her waist and she leaned back against me.

Jimmy Van Dan and his Perfect Strangers were a group of five guys in their late twenties. They wore early-Beatles shirts—striped with white collars. Jimmy

Van Dan, who introduced himself and the group, had a black high-collared shirt on. He had his sleeves rolled up and wore a light beige tie and khaki pants. I wanted clothes like that. I never have any clothes.

Jimmy Van Dan had a good stage attitude—the audience seemed more concerned about whether or not he would like them, rather than the other way around.

"This is the first tune, it's called 'Non-Fiction.' One, a-two, a-one, two, three, four."

Canada and I moved closer to the bandstand and after the start of the second song, "Found Money," we started dancing with each other. Practically the whole crowd was dancing. We were doing like a bop or some kind of early American Bandstand stuff. That's what the music was like. Like "Let's Go to the Hop." Canada moved in and out around me as we danced. It was like we had danced together before. We could really hear the music and stay inside the beat. It was exciting. It felt as if I was feeling her breast when I was only touching her hand.

Next the band did "Where or When," the old ballad. "We always play this next tune on date nights," Jimmy Van Dan said. They did it slow, and Jimmy Van Dan sang it beautifully, with no kidding around. It was right and it was romantic. Near the end of the song Canada and I kissed again. We went back to the bar to get our beers and look around for Jack. We looked all over the place for him and finally spotted him talking to a guy with shoulder-length frizzy black hair topped with a red beret.

"I wouldn't mind leaving. Would you like to go? We can stay if you want," I said loudly into Canada's ear.

"I'd like to go if you would."

"I would." Then, "Jack," I yelled.

He turned around. "What do you think of them?"

"They're great."

"Yeah, really great, Jack," Canada said.

Jack turned and whispered something to the red bereted guy then said to us, "You guys want to go to a party? We're leavin' here now. You want to go?"

"I don't really feel like going. Would you like to go?" I said to Canada.

"I don't really feel like going."

"You sure?"

She shook her head and took my hand. I yelled up to Jack. "Jack, we're finished. You go. You young people go."

He gave me a disappointed look then laughed. He leaned over the railing and asked Canada if she'd be okay.

"Oh, sure, Jack. Sandy'll take me home."

He smiled down at us both and wiggled his eyebrows like Groucho Marx. He turned to go. I yelled up to him and he turned around. "Thank you, Jack," I said. "Thank you for the night."

He looked at me, waited a second, and then said, "*Mi casa, su casa,*" and disappeared.

We finally made it through the crowd and out into the cold.

"Could it be colder, please," I shouted straight up. "Jesus, let's go straight to the airport, go to Miami, buy a condo, rub some white stuff on our noses, and lie down in our cabana clothes."

She put her arm around me and rubbed her little hand up and down my back to warm me up.

"Thank you. You know," I said, "this has been the nicest night. The last few days have been rough. This is the nicest night I could have had. I'm really glad I met you. I'm really so glad Jack brought you by. Remind me to cut Jack a check."

She laughed. "I'm glad he brought me by too."

"Just for the dancing alone," I said. "I really like dancing with you."

"We dance well together. Sandy, are you going with someone? I wasn't going to ask that, or at least I wasn't going to ask you right away. But then I thought, why shouldn't I?"

"No, it's okay that you asked. I was thinking the same thing about you. No, I'm not going with anybody. I was sort of seeing somebody, but now I'm sort of doing it alone, as they say." We missed getting a cab. "How about you? Are you married to a Mafia chieftain or anything I should know about?"

She laughed. "No. I was married to a guy in the FBI, though."

"You're kidding me."

"Yeah, I'm kidding."

"Don't do that," I told her. "If I have a stroke in this neighborhood they'll bury me a Catholic. No, seriously Canada, are you going with someone? You probably are, huh?"

"No, I'm not. I was going with a guy who's in Europe now. He works with his father in the import business. He set up an office or something in Paris and now he's living there. It was sort of over before he left anyway. It's his apartment I've got. Actually it's his older brother's apartment, but Stephen set it up for me to sublet it on a month-to-month thing."

"The apartment over the Big Wok?"

"Uh-huh."

"How are you feeling? Are you freezing?"

"No, are you?"

Her apartment wasn't very decorated. There was a large poster of Elvis Costello over the fireplace, a few pieces of furniture—a couch, a table and one chair, a stool, and a double bed on the floor by the window. It was a studio, and the spareness gave the room a clean look. The walls were fresh white and all her personal things were laid out neatly. On a low table by the bed there was an old-fashioned powderpuff box with two sets of gold earrings in it and a silver hairbrush lying on its back with a tortoiseshell comb stuck lengthwise into the bristles. The few plates and cups were all washed and turned upside down on paper towels in the kitchenette—to keep the roaches out, I guess.

Canada asked me for my coat and hung it up with hers on a hanger in the narrow closet. As far as I could tell, there didn't seem to be any men's clothes in there. On the mantel of the bricked-in fireplace was a fifties' yellow plastic radio with red dials, and tucked into the mirror was a strip of those arcade four-for-a-dollar photographs. They were of Canada and a young, good-looking guy with dark hair wearing sunglasses. They were in the usual poses—the guy giving the finger to the camera, the two of them making monster faces, him pushing her out of the shot, and one of them kissing.

She went to the stereo and slowly leaned down over a large record collection. She picked out the Joni Mitchell "Blue" album.

"I love that old record," I told her. "It's got one of the best songs ever written on it."

" 'A Case of You'?"

"Yeah."

"I love it too."

She put the record on at the perfect volume, then turned on a little china lamp by the bed. Then she went over to the door and clicked off the overhead light.

"Okay?" she said.

"Yeah."

She smiled at me and sat on the bed. I sat down on one of the chairs by the fireplace.

Canada was pulling off her winter boots.

"I can never get these things off," she said.

I asked her if she needed a hand, but she got them off.

"Can I take my boots off too or do you think you'll lose all respect for me?" I asked.

"Take them off and risk it," she said.

I laughed and she laughed. I pulled off my boots and put them neatly next to the chair I was sitting on. "I like this apartment, Canada."

"It's pretty empty now. I'd like to fix it up, but I don't really have that much stuff."

"Well, you'll get stuff. New York City is the stuff capital of the world."

"Yeah," she said, "I guess it is."

There was a pause in which I looked around again. And when I looked back at her sitting there on the bed she was rubbing her short hair off her forehead with the heel of her hand. And when she saw me looking at her she didn't look away.

I said, "You're very beautiful."

All she did was tilt her head to the right and cast her eyes down. I sat on the bed next to her.

"Is this okay?" I asked.

"Yes."

She cupped my hand in both of hers and breathed in deeply. Her full breasts rose up under her thin black sweater.

Suddenly I knew that if I went to bed with Canada "our boy" would be impotent. (I know this makes bad reading, but it's what I thought.) I hadn't felt such idiotic panic for years because I'd wised up enough not to pursue women who made me nervous enough to be impotent. And the truth was, Canada didn't make me nervous in that way either. No, that was clear. It was another thing entirely.

It was Mary.

My nervous system was shot. The impotence was just a bad reaction to everything but it panicked me. I knew I should stop the evening before I went too far. I didn't need the added guilt and embarrassment of apologizing nude, holding an empty condom.

I was at least smart enough not to fool around with myself. By that I mean, I didn't kiss Canada again just to see if I could bluff my genitals into performing.

"You're really great, Canada, I like you. I've had a real nice time tonight. And you and Jack coming over like that was a real rescue at sea." I got up and walked across the room.

"I had a great time too," she said.

"I'd like to see you again," I told her. "You know, if you want to sometime."

"I would."

I walked in a small circle.

"Are you okay, Sandy?"

She put her little hand on my shoulder.

"It's nothing that I can't handle," I said optimistically. "You know, Canada, a friend of mine passed away recently. I'm having trouble filing it away."

"That can be the hardest thing," she said. "I didn't know. I mean, I couldn't tell you were . . ."

"Yeah, well, I'll go along fine, you know, and then this friend, you see, tried to get in touch with me before they . . . You know what I probably need, Canada, is some sleep."

I didn't know what I was saying at that point. I just wanted to be legit without using Mary to make a legend out of myself. On guard, on constant guard.

"Maybe I'll just go home and crash. I've had such a good time, though."

She moved over to me and kissed my mouth. I kissed her back. My heart started jumping but it wasn't jumping out of the good stuff.

"Can I take your phone number?" I asked her, feeling like a wimp.

"Sure," she said. "Let me take yours too."

She clicked on the overhead light again, which made things even more depressing. She tore off a piece of the *Village Voice* and wrote her number down on it. Then she opened up her address book and took mine. I put my coat on while we walked toward the door. She was being nice. I tried not to think that she really thought I was just making my dead friend up.

"Sandy, if you want to talk to anyone or you need someone to keep you company, give me a call, you know?"

"That's very kind of you."

She was tucking my scarf around my neck.

"I mean it," she said lifting my chin up to meet her eyes.

"Thank you, kiddo. Thanks a lot."

I kissed her on the mouth and then on the cheek. She opened the door and I went out into the hall. I turned and headed for the stairs.

"Be careful," she whispered.

I moved down the stairs feeling glad that I had handled my insanity in a healthy manner. I could call Canada again sometime if I ever wound up feeling any better, and she probably wouldn't give me the brush. But by the time I reached the front door and was out on the street I wasn't thinking of anyone but myself—as usual. It seemed that with every hour since Monday, I'd grown darker inside. As I walked along Greenwich Street I thought again about my panic in Canada's room. It wasn't a throwback to my early, gun-slinging Casanova days. I knew that. I wasn't afraid to sleep with this beautiful, Leslie Caronesque girl because I was afraid I wouldn't impress her properly and not make a fan out of her. No. I was afraid that in the darkness of her bed she'd physically be Mary.

I had started "going" with Mary again the moment I got her letter, and I couldn't be unfaithful.

It was terribly cold and my big ears had almost dropped off my head by the time I got to my place. I turned the oven on for extra heat, having no phoney log for the fireplace. It was about three-thirty or so in the morning. Mary's note was on the table in the living room. I walked toward it and stopped. I got out of my clothes and into my big winter bathrobe.

One time, about a week after Mary and I said we loved each other, she gave me a key to her apartment. That night she wanted to finish some work for that mean woman on Fifty-seventh Street. It wasn't enough that she was working eighty-seven hours a day for her, she also had to bring work home. Anyway, she had given me the key that day and had told me to go off with the boys that night. So I went uptown to the comedy club and stayed till two in the morning, smoking dope and drinking with some stand-up comic friends of mine. I started flirting with a Mexican waitress who worked there and went back to her place and had sex with her. I got back to Mary's apartment around five in the morning. I fooled around with the key in the lock for about half an hour trying to get the door open. I finally got in and Mary just half woke up. And beautiful guy that I am, I then went into the bathroom and washed myself so Mary wouldn't find the scent of another woman on me. And then I climbed into bed with her.

"Honey, did I wake you up?" I asked her.

She shook her head and kissed me.

"Richard and I went out to eat after he finished at the club and—"

"I love you," she said and went back to sleep.

I went back into my living room and stared at Mary's letter from six feet away. I pulled my emergency cigarettes out of the drawer and lit one up. When

I smoked half of it I lit up another. I sat down on the couch and reread her letter.

It's nothing you've done, but it feels like it is.

The cigarette started it off. I was going to throw up. I didn't even make it to the bathroom. I barely made it to the kitchen sink. Stuff came up from 1958. I heaved for what felt like an hour. Everything came up but my guilt. Close to dawn I finished cleaning out the sink and spraying it with Lysol. I brushed my teeth and wiped the sick tears out of my eyes and went to bed. I don't remember dreaming.

SATURDAY

"Hello?"
"Ansil, hi, this is Sandy Bayard."
"Hi, Sandy."
"Hi."
"How are you doin'?"
"Not bad."
"So Ansil," I said, "here's what I'm gonna do. I'm gonna buy a gun and give it to you and you can shoot me, so you won't be so mad at me anymore."
"I'm not mad at you, Sandy."
"Well, I deserve to be somewhat mad at."
I picked up the base of the phone and started pac-

ing around my living room. My heart was doing a clog dance.

"Ansil, am I catching you at a bad time? Can you talk a little bit now, or what?"

"It's okay."

"Well, I'd very much like to see you and talk with you a little. I wouldn't blame you if you told me no, but I'd really like to see you. I've been going through a lot of things. I'm a little nuts, and—"

"Okay."

"—and, if you prefer not to get together I'd understand. What?"

"Let's get together. It's okay."

"It's all right?"

"Yeah."

"Good," I said. "Anyway, Ansil, we were havin' a couple of laughs that night before you insulted me and walked out."

Ansil let out a mild chuckle and said, "Yeah, sometimes I run off too much at the mouth."

"Well," I told him, "I've never had that problem but I can imagine it probably offends people."

"Sandy, I have to go now, but what are you doing in about an hour?"

"Nothing. I'm an open person."

"Well, I've got to stop at the B.B. Hayes Gallery. The B.B. Hayes Gallery on West Broadway?"

"Down in SoHo?"

"Right. Why don't you come by there in about an hour?"

"Great. Thanks, Ansil. I appreciate it."

"Okay," he said. "I'll see you then, huh?"

"Yeah, great. I'll see you then, Ansil."

We hung up. I stared at my phone for about an hour or so. It was about eleven A.M.

I got to the B.B. Hayes Gallery at noon. You walk right into it off the street. A lot of sunlight in the place. I saw Ansil right away. He was hammering the devil out of a wooden platform. The only other person in the place was a very sexy woman with red hair. She wore white overalls and a pink polo shirt.

"Yes?" she said to me as if I was tracking blood into the joint.

"He's a friend of mine, Rose," Ansil said. He nodded and smiled at me. "Where's that gun you promised me, Sandy?"

I laughed and Rose turned around.

"He's kidding, Rose. He's kidding," I said.

She shook her head like she didn't know what we two kookballs were up to. I slid down the wall and sat on the floor next to where Ansil was working.

He hammered a few times then said, "I'm glad you came down Sandy."

I looked to see where Rose was. And then I said, "Just before Mary died she sent me a short letter."

He stopped his hammer halfway to the nail. Ansil got off his knee, waited, and then slid down the wall and sat next to me. We were both facing the same way.

"This is it," I said. I took the letter out of my back pocket and handed it to him. He took a long pause and then opened it. I hadn't thought of bringing the letter up so quickly but before I left home I decided the best thing was not to worry too much about the best way to handle things.

"It's weird," he said.

"Yeah," I said. "Maybe *the* weirdest thing."

He read it again and handed it back to me. Then I read it again, then he read it again over my shoulder.

"What do you think it means?" he said.

I shook my head. We just looked straight ahead. Rose was looking at us from about thirty feet away.

"I've been trying all kinds of ways to find out what it means," I said. "I've been wracking my brain, I swear to God. You know, Ansil, I tried to be totally nice to Mary, I think. I can't say that about too many other girls I've gone with, but I did try to be nice to her. I even went to Boston after I got this."

"You did?"

"Yeah. Her father tried to strangle me. Not really, but . . ."

He smiled a little.

"Maybe I shouldn't have come to see you, Ansil, you know?"

"No, no."

"Really?"

"I wanted to see you."

"You know, it's really killing me, Ansil. I can't figure it out. If I did something . . ."

I stopped talking because I was afraid my voice might get wobbly. Rose was coming toward us anyway.

"Let's get out of here and get a drink," Ansil said.

I hadn't heard him.

"Huh?"

"I said, let's get some whiskey." He was already standing. He reached his long arm down and took my hand and pulled me up.

"Rose, I'll meet you back at your place, okay?" he said.

"I thought we were going to pick up stuff for dinner," she said.

"Well, could you pick it up? I'll meet you back at your place after a while."

"When?"

"After a while."

Ansil asked me if I minded if we went back to the Broome Street Bar.

I said, "No. After all, that's *our* place."

When we left the gallery Ansil took out a cigarette and gave me one. We stopped for half a second while he lit us up. Sensually dressed housewives walked by with their husbands.

"You don't think you know what she meant, do you, man?" I asked Ansil.

"No, I don't. Let's get a drink."

The Broome Street was filled for lunch. We sat at the bar. There was a section in the corner that was empty.

"Hey, Sandy, you famous yet?"

It was Johnny May. He also worked days.

"Still no more famous than I was a week ago, Johnny May."

"Well, get famous. I can't wait forever."

"Okay."

"What do you guys want?"

Ansil ordered. "Two beers, two shots of Wild Turkey." He looked at me. "Okay?"

"Good."

Johnny went to get the drinks. We took off our coats and hung them on the rack at the corner of the bar. Johnny came back with the drinks.

Ansil snubbed out the cigarette he had started on the street. Mine had gone out by itself. We each took large swigs of whiskey and big gulps of beer. The usual pretty crowd was in the restaurant.

"I don't know what that note meant, Sandy, to tell you the truth."

He lit another cigarette.

"Yeah. No," I said, "it's hard to under—"

"No, I don't know what it means."

I took the rest of my whiskey and a sip of beer.

"Uh, is Rose a girlfriend, Ansil?" I asked. That's all I could think of to say.

"What?"

"She's nice."

"No. I just met her again. I mean, I knew her a few years ago at school. But I just met her again."

He gave out a little breath and shrugged his shoulders. He finished his whiskey and took some beer.

"I can't say why she might have written that note to you, Sandy. It's hard to even think about it, to tell you the truth."

"Yeah, yes, I know it must be, Ansil, and I'm sorry . . . I sort of wish I hadn't . . . you know, I . . ."

Ansil got up and put a bunch of bills down on the bar. He put his coat on. We said something back and forth to each other about being in touch or some such bullshit, but I knew that unless I ran into him somewhere, I'd never see him again. He walked to the door, stopped, turned around, and came back. He stood there looking down at me and then he reached his right hand into his coat pocket. Don't forget, I was nuts at the time, so in that fraction of a second I thought he was going to pull out a gun. He didn't; he pulled out his keys. He pulled two keys off the ring and put them on the bar in front of me.

"This is the key to her place, Sandy. Mary's apartment. All she ever did was write. Maybe there's something in all of it that might help you . . . I don't know." He pointed to the keys. "One's to the building and the other's to her front door."

"Ansil."

"Yeah."

"Thank you."

He nodded.

"No," I said, touching his hand. "I mean it. This is kind of you to do this."

He nodded again and said, "It may do you no good."

I thanked him again. He didn't, or couldn't, say anything more. And then he left. I thought about whether or not I'd have given him the keys if the situation had been reversed. I probably wouldn't have. There's every possibility *I'd* have let someone who slept with my lover suffer. There was no question Ansil was doing a generous thing. And as strange as it sounds, I also believed he was doing it out of anger over her having written me anything at all.

I took a cab to Mary's place on Charles Street. My heart was pounding and I was sweating and hot even though it had gotten several degrees colder in the few minutes Ansil and I had been in the bar.

I tried both keys about a thousand times on the building lock until one of them turned it. I had been leaning on the door so when it finally opened I fell into the hallway, practically crushing some old lady about to walk her dog. The dog didn't even notice, it was so anxious to get outside. I apologized a lot to the old lady, who just looked at me as if I were a juvenile delinquent. I waited until she went out and then walked up Mary's stairway. I swear to God I was in better shape than I thought because my heart was thumping hard enough to give a stroke. I walked up the steps one at a time, trying to slow my heart down, but that just seemed to speed it up. I tried to make myself get mad, hoping that would stop the fear I was feeling. I started talking to my heart. "Okay, you bastard! Burst! You'd be doing me a favor!"

My hand was shaking as I aimed the key at her door. It took my other hand helping to get it in the lock and turned. I opened the door slowly. "Mary, please don't let your ghost be in here."

Her room was the same. The window over the radiator was open and there was a cold wind blowing through. Just as I got to the window and closed it, her cat Entropy screeched out at me from nowhere. He was wild-eyed and crazed. Nobody'd come round to feed him. I rolled up a magazine in case he went for me and opened a can of food. He gulped it down like a lunatic, looking over his shoulder at me a bunch of times. He didn't look that skinny or weak, just mad. I stood at the window looking around, just waiting for the room to warm up. I don't know why, but I'd thought her inanimate things would look different now that she was dead. There was a box of Q-tips on her dresser. I stared at them for a while. God! A box of Q-tips had outlived her. I guess I should have been shocked that none of her family had come to claim her belongings.

The radiator was coughing up a little heat. A stack of her poems was sitting in a neat pile on her typing desk, but I didn't go for them yet. Instead I went to her closet, opened the door, and looked at her clothes. I put a sleeve of a corduroy jacket to my face. I turned my back and over my shoulder looked at the poems. Then I felt the coat again. I remembered buttoning it for her once, just as she came out of her front door to meet me. We were on our way to the movies or someplace.

I took a deep breath, walked to the still-open door and locked it. I shook my head and went to the desk. There was a stack of blank paper waiting to be written on to the left of the old Olivetti. To the right of the typewriter was a stack of poems about half an inch high. I started looking for a poem entitled "Why I Sent Bayard the Note." The one on top was about Ansil's body. In the Ansil poem she referred a lot to their skins. Hers as grey. The few poems after that used characters from Greek mythology—Cyclops, Phoenixes. There was a beautiful one about her watching the mounted police ride past her window on Hudson Street and of her wanting one of them to wear her colors. But from there the writing was only black, with no one but herself in any of it. The last one was the scariest. It was about the sun not setting and what the heat did to her. I couldn't finish it. I began to smell her burning in the words.

I pushed myself away from the desk and opened the window a crack for some air. Next to the window, on a little shelf, was a picture of Mary at the ocean, floating on her back in the water. I pulled the picture closer. Her eyes were wide open and happy. She was yelling something to someone. I just stared at her. Her eyes. The picture must have been taken last summer after she and I stopped seeing each other. And the thing that kept hitting me about it was that she had grown much more beautiful. I wasn't imagining it, it was almost a structural change in the face. It was frightening and perverse in a way. Her chemistry seemed to be drawing an ever-increasing distinction between her body and her soul.

I put the picture back on its shelf and looked around for more of her writing. I remember there used to be poems and stories all over the place. Maybe Ansil had taken some and not told me, or maybe Mary had destroyed some knowing she was going to kill herself. On the floor near the fireplace was her old red briefcase. But there was only a train timetable for Long Island in it. Next to her fireplace was her portable stereo. She had left it on. There was no record on the turntable but it was going around anyway.

I reached over and clicked it off and a hum I hadn't noticed before went out of the room. I sat down on the floor and leaned against the old bricks of the fireplace. I looked from one end of the small room to the other, wondering how it could have contained the volume of her fear for as long as it had. Sitting there, in that corner, I could almost see the perimeters of her despair. I physically felt the edges of it.

It had gotten very warm. I still had my overcoat on. I stood up, took my coat off, and laid it on the bed. I walked to the dresser and opened the top drawer. A perfumed lavender sachet was next to her handkerchiefs.

I heard the clip-clopping of the Eighth Avenue police horses heading home. I looked down at them as if they were my reflection in a brook—the big Irish cops laughing like the twenty-three year olds they were. My self-hatred lasted six days, and that shamed me in a way.

I put Mary's sachet in my pocket. I was laughing—as bad as that sounds to say it. Maybe it was the smell of the sachet—I had been holding onto it as though it were Mary's hand.

I wondered who would move into her place. I wondered whether whoever it was, a guy who'd just split up with his wife maybe, would feel the pain hovering around in this studio with an alcove—pain like an ancient and mythic humidity. Somebody I know once played poker in the house where Manson murdered those people. The whole night he felt something badder and bigger than what he could see. They only told him where he was after the game.

God, she had the real thing, the real pain. I could feel it. Could I feel it so strongly if I had contributed to it? And at that moment I knew I was a good enough guy. The winter light brightened in movement across the room, and with it my heart cleared as if a leper had gotten his miracle.

The buzzer screamed in the room. Entropy kept on eating and making groaning sounds. My breath whistled in my lungs. The buzzer went of again. It could've been Mary's ghost or a lion and I wouldn't have been afraid. I pushed the button by the door, the building door swung open below, and I could hear girls laughing deep in the distance, footsteps getting stronger, coming upstairs slowly. I went out on the landing and waited.

"Sandy, I have to talk to you."

Ansil stood still when he got to where I was, out of breath, but not from expending energy. I nodded my head once and he followed me back inside. Entropy padded out of the kitchenette and gave us a disgusted look. Ansil took off his cheap, hip European overcoat, ran his hand jerkily through his hair.

"Her cat. Everybody forgot her cat." He said it like it was a poem.

I kept looking at him. It wasn't in the look, but I wanted to kill him. It was strange, no anger or anything, but if this had been a war and I was one of those elite forces guys I could've killed him, so subtly. He had a thing folded up in his hand. He passed in front of me and opened the window wider, looked back around, then closed the window completely. He looked down at his hand. The thing was a blue piece of paper folded the long way, the same color with the same red lines across it as Mary's note.

"I tried to call you, Sandy. The next morning, after that night at Ann's, I called you several times . . ."

"I was away." I sat there with yoga clarity on the bed Mary grew up on.

He unfolded the sheet of paper and looked at it. In the sunlight over his shoulder I could see Mary's handwriting through the page.

"I feel terrible, Sandy. I . . . I had the letter on me Monday night down at the Broome Street." He sat on a corner of the radiator cover. "The couple of lines you found in your apartment house door was all that was on the second page of her note. This is the first page."

"You put it on my door?"

He nodded yes. "I took the page out and then put it on your door." Then he told me Mary had written it in Boston and her father's wife had given it to him along with some of her stuff.

He told me again how he had it on him that night before we went up to Ann's.

"I got drunk and then you said how I should have stood up for her more. When I left Ann's apartment I freaked out and got drunker and . . . she wrote this to *you*." He got up to look out the window. "I wanted to hurt you."

I slid the letter away from him, then I went out into the hallway and sat on her steps.

    Dearest Ralph, Pal O'mine,
Riding your bus down Madison avenue,
    sharing yard-long Heros and bowling nights like
        God,
happiness flew through me like golden blood.
But the sad-beauty part, brother Raccoon, is that
        even
30 minutes of happiness in black and white, to an
"underwater engineer" like your old Pal Norton is
        like . . .
    somebody's little mad child momentarily
understanding his madness and the oncoming
red darkness rolling in.
My hands are too wet to hold onto you my dear
        friend.
Too many old colors that will not wait.
So think of me when next you pass Raccoon Point,
        wave

your cap for me, wear your funny eyes at the convention
and don't be sad my darling friend you did not invent
happiness—

The letter in my hand ended here, the one in my pocket went on: "It's nothing you did, but it feels like it is."

Mary's cat came up and sat in my lap. I folded the two pages together, lifted my sweater, and tucked the poem into my shirt pocket. Ansil was in the doorway looking at me. I suppose there was some big feeling on his face. Entropy was purring.

"Do you think Mary has one of those things?"

"Huh?"

"One of those cat suitcases. Maybe I'll take it with me for a while."

"Yeah, she has one."

He went back inside. I took a deep breath and pulled me and the cat to our feet. Ansil was reaching high up over the kitchen cabinets and brought down a plaid carrying case. Entropy tensed but we got him in there and closed the door. Ansil didn't talk to me. He didn't ask me anything.

"Why don't you give all her poems to her brother," I said.

He nodded.

Steam heat came up through the radiator like it has and always will. I put the cat down on the desk and looked around the place for the last time, then I walked over to Ansil and hit him as hard as I could. I had to reach up to do it. He grabbed his face and rubber-legged into her desk knocking her poems all over the place. I was ready for him to rip my head off. He had a thin red welt coming up across his cheek to his ear. I felt like my knuckles were pushed back to my elbow. He got set to come for me, but relaxed.

"Take the cat home, Sandy." He pulled himself up on the corner of the bed. "It's over, take her cat home."

Things stayed like that for a few minutes. He dropped his eyes. He was the saddest grown-up man I ever saw.

"You can hit me, Ansil, you could knock me unconscious."

Then he turned toward a whole new bunch of sunlight coming into the room. A tear came out of his eye.

"The world is the hardest planet . . ." I said, and sat down on the corner of the bed. Ansil swallowed hard, as if kids had made fun of him in the schoolyard. I held my right hand up. It had swelled up into one of those joke store hands. "I'm sending you the bill for this."

Jesus it hurt. What was he waiting for? Why didn't he leave?

"You okay?" He was sincerely concerned.

"Never once, not ever, has anything been remotely like the movies for me!"

There was another long pause. Ansil got up. I braced to be hit, but he went into the kitchen and returned with a bottle of blackberry brandy and two ruby-colored *Little Women*–delicate wine goblets.

He poured us some brandy and sat down, putting the bottle between us. I had an image of some belle in the Civil War building her entrance by keeping rival suitors waiting.

We sat there silently for close to eight or ten minutes. We drank two more glasses apiece. After the next one, I proposed a good-bye toast to Mary's bathroom mirror.

"A lot of mirrors have to have pimply guys from

the ad business shave before them, here's to the mirror that Mary powdered in."

Then Ansil toasted Mary's Stevie Wonder's "Greatest Hits" album.

I raised a glass to her window ledge. She had once yelled the kind of Chinese food she wanted me to bring back to her from it. Together we ended up toasting the white wrought-iron table and chairs in the kitchen, a little silhouette of Mary as a kid, her profile cut out of black paper laid against white. An oar with her brother's name on it from a summer camp, and all her hardcover books. "Hardcover books are such a luxury," she had said. We even drank one to pictures of her mother and father in separate frames on her desk. She would've been happy about us doing that.

Then Ansil and I stood at the two big windows and looked down at the young policemen riding their golden brown horses.

"You want to come see the cat, Ansil, you call me and come see it."

"Okay."

I stood and went to the door.

"You call me and come see it."

He nodded yes.

SUNDAY

I took a boat ride around Manhattan. It was a little before noon, sixty degrees, and the sun was turning the city into a boutonniere in God's lapel. I bought a warm cheese Danish, and no one can touch that Circle Line coffee. It's funny how I never have really believed in life's deeper pleasures. The grand pleasures, ones that Shakespeare might write a whole play around. I thought believing in that happened to people on one or the other extreme of life. Not for basically lucky people in the middle like me. I was on the open top part of the boat. Just me and an English family. The young husband and wife loved being with each other and the two little girls seemed to enjoy being well behaved.

One Halloween I was too sick to go out and trick or treat. My mother sprinkled her perfume on a quilt and made me up a bed on the couch in the Florida room. I remember I was watching "Attack of the Puppet People" on the big old black and white TV when the front door opened wide. My mother was sitting behind me sweeping my hair off my forehead slowly, rhythmically, but she bolted when the door opened because my dad was away, he was off selling neckties through the Southern states. Driving his '53 Buick, making buyers genuinely laugh. But it was my dad at the door. He'd left the car up in Augusta and had spent a lot of his commission dough on a one-night flight home. And I remember the bay rum and his tan and blue oxford shirt and the look on his face. Young as I was I knew he was mad at God or whatever for making me sick again, and as much trouble as it was for him, he was defying the bad luck that had the balls to make his little boy sad. He improvised some Halloween stuff for my face and, still in the quilt, he carried me to every house in the neighborhood. As we moved through the humid night wind, I expected at any moment my father might decide to stop doing business with the sidewalk and float us up above everything. As soon as we got home with the candy, he had to go right back to the airport. There were two more weeks of Beau Brummell ties to sell. More than anything that happened that night, I'll never forget how much my mother loved my father right then. For her, he was the guy.

I'm not saying I was even half the guy for Mary. I wasn't. But for a while I was something. And who knows how long one must live to get the idea. Even if I had died young, I still would have gotten the idea about part of all of this from that look on my mother's face.

When the boat started making its last turn around the city, a tall girl, a model type, walked up on the top deck. She had a kind of dark look in her eye, as if she had given her boyfriend this Sunday to "make up his mind."